BOY ON THE WIRE

ALSO BY ALASTAIR BRUCE

Wall of Days

BOY ON THE WIRE

THE CLERKENWELL PRESS

First published in Great Britain in 2015 by
The Clerkenwell Press
an imprint of
PROFILE BOOKS LTD
3 Holford Yard
Bevin Way
London WC1X 9HD
www.profilebooks.com

1 3 5 7 9 10 8 6 4 2

Printed and bound in Great Britain by
Clays Ltd, St Ives Plc

The moral right of the author has been asserted.

A CIP catalogue record for this book is available from the British Library.

ISBN 978 1 78125 454 7
eISBN 978 1 78283 161 7

FSC
www.fsc.org
MIX
Paper from
responsible sources
FSC® C018072

For my family

Prologue

December 2011

Cape Road leads from the centre of Port Elizabeth, near the cricket ground, west into the suburbs. At the national road it branches south and the tarmac becomes narrower as it leads away from the city. The houses grow larger and are set further and further back from the road. Some are invisible behind the blue gum trees. If you follow this road for about twenty minutes, until after the streetlights end, you will come first to a single-storey house, painted white, but now brown with dust. There is a light on in the lounge of this house. Next door is a larger house, two storeys, built out of red-brick. This house is in darkness, save for a single light over the front door.

John Hyde sits in a chair in the bungalow. The patio door is open and the drawn curtains shift in the breeze.

There is a full moon. The moonlight gets in between the gap in the curtains and washes over Hyde's face. The light seems to wipe his features away.

His hands rest on the arms of the chair. The upholstery is sticky. Sweat, dirt from other people, people he does not know. His fingers are curled as if he wants to scratch the chair, but he does not move them. He has been still for some time.

Hyde stares ahead. Against the wall is a television and a laptop is on the floor in front of it. There is a stack of discs on the floor. Most have dates written on them, a few are still in their wrappers.

In the laptop is a disc with yesterday's date on it. Hyde is watching this in black and white. He sees a figure facing away from the camera, standing in the middle of a room in front of a mirror. The figure in the mirror looks back towards the camera but the face is blurred.

The television gives off a low buzz, but that is the only sound. When the man on the screen opens his mouth, nothing is heard. There is only a picture of a man with his mouth moving, skin stretched over his face.

Hyde gets out of the chair and goes into the garden. He looks up at the stars, leaning his head back as far as it will go. He has not seen stars like this since the last time he was in this country, eighteen years ago.

He turns his head and begins walking. He walks up the drive, out to the road, and along to the house next door. He freezes when opposite it, thinking he has seen someone in a window. He stares at the window for a long time. He can see a man there, or he imagines he can see a man.

Something twitches inside him: a memory of a boy standing at the same window, watching a woman – his mother – as she drives away. He feels this twitch like a creature with spines unsheathing inside him.

He pushes at the gate and it swings open. The noise goes through him. He waits before stepping in. A minute. He scans the windows, but there is nothing.

He moves to his right and walks along the fence that separates the larger house from the bungalow. It is darker here in the shadows of the trees. He walks to the closest point to the house and stops. All is quiet. From here he can see the garage and through a window into the kitchen and another top-storey window into one of the bedrooms.

After a while he approaches the house. In his pocket is a key to the kitchen door. He places it in the lock, turns it. It has not been bolted from the inside. He steps in and shuts the door quietly after him.

He knows the house well. He has been staying here when not in the bungalow: it is the house in which he grew up. All the same, he feels like an intruder.

The carpets have been stripped, leaving the stairs bare concrete, and each footstep echoes through the house. At the top of the stairs is an iron security gate. Hyde takes one step at a time, leading always with his right leg. The gate bolt is shot. He begins to draw it back, tries to stop it touching metal. Like a child's game. He stops every time the metal scrapes, and listens but hears nothing.

Hyde stands, the open gate before him, on the final step. He peers around the wall to his right towards the main bedroom. The door is ajar, though it is black beyond. He waits, leaning his head against the wall. He looks straight ahead through the open door of another bedroom and out of the window. A light moves across the sky. An aeroplane. The outside world. He stares until it disappears.

At the main bedroom door, he stops again. He hears breathing, whether his own or someone else's, he cannot tell. It is soft. Perhaps not breath but the wind.

He pushes the door open another few inches and sees a foot, a leg, a torso. A thin shaft of moonlight lies over the face, over one eye. Hyde jerks his head back.

When he looks again, the body lies stretched on the bed, the chest rising and falling evenly. Hyde feels sick standing there watching this, feels a black sick rise in him.

He marvels, too, at the extent of his deception. Here he is, guilty, in plain view. He knows, too, he cannot touch him, cannot touch the lying man. If he even touched the tip of his fingers to the man's forehead, it would all be over.

There are photographs on the bedside table. He flips through them. The first shows a boy crouching in the bush, his back to the camera, a small boy trying to be smaller still.

In the second are three boys, the older two with their arms around each other, grinning, the youngest standing in the background. They are in a valley, surrounded by mountains. There is a date on the back: 11 December 1983.

The last shows two of the boys from the previous photograph. They crouch before something in the road – a dead animal. The arm of one of the boys, the eldest of the three, is around the shoulder of the smallest child – or on the shoulder. Pushing or pulling, it is not clear.

Hyde has seen these photographs before. He took one of them, in fact, many years ago. Though he looks at them for some time, he shows no reaction.

He goes out of the room and walks along the corridor. He is about to enter the bedroom furthest away from the main bedroom when he stops. There are footsteps behind him. The concrete of the passageway amplifies the noise, but it seems to have begun right behind him. He feels his neck tingle and turns slowly. There, framed in the doorway, standing still, is the man he has been watching, his head hanging down, arms at his sides. Scarecrow. One arm reaches for the frame and the man's fingernails begin to tap at it. The sound goes through Hyde, who has not moved.

He watches the man, who now walks right up to him. Hyde can smell him, the stink of him. He walks backwards as the other walks towards him – almost, he feels, into him – slipping under the skin of him. Hyde closes his eyes for a moment and feels the heat of the other, feels his breath on him.

It is not this that troubles him, the proximity of this figure, but it is the way the man looks. Now, with the moonlight full on the man's face, Hyde can see, though it is exactly as he expected, what he most fears. It is not a shock. Somewhere he has enough left in him not to be surprised, to know the true meaning of the man opposite him, the truth of his guilt.

He is a man who lied, who told a story, a wild, fanciful story, about the death of a child, a hard and unyielding story.

It is that, he finds, that he hates most. The story that was told.

Standing this close to the man, looking into his eyes, the scar on his chin from a fall, his familiar smell, John Hyde knows now what he has done. And there is no going back from this.

1

It is a Sunday, the eleventh of December 1983, a day the boy has looked forward to for some time. His head hangs out of the window. He feels the wind in his face and twists his neck so the wind blows his hair backwards, then to the sides. His hair tickles his forehead. His face will feel warm later from the wind and sunburn. He has freckles on his nose that will disappear as his skin grows darker in the sun.

From inside the car he hears a voice telling him to pull his head in. He ignores it and does not hear it again. The voice had not sounded urgent, as if the speaker was only saying it because he felt he had to, not because he meant it. It is the holidays after all and they are on their way to a cottage they have rented in the mountains of the Karoo.

The Chevrolet has brown plastic seats which stick to the boy's skin and the tiny holes in the plastic leave an imprint on his legs. He runs his fingers over the bumps.

The back of his hand brushes against the leg of another boy, an older one, sitting in the middle seat, who knocks it away with his leg. Still, the younger boy does not pull his head in.

He looks at the fields rolling past. They seem almost endless, stretching off to mountains in the distance. The fields are different colours, some like beach sand, others grey. He thinks of these as the surface of the moon. He imagines what it would be like to be in the middle of one of the fields now. Silence. An ant scuttling over his toe. In the field he turns his head and in the distance sees a car on the national road. He cannot hear it – only see it – and when the sun catches the car at the wrong angle, he is blinded for a second. He cannot see inside, but can see the boy's head, his own, hanging out of the window. He feels their eyes lock for a moment. Then the car disappears, and he is alone, and he thinks that if he goes into the gully where the grass is a bit longer, he could sleep, and with the water in the animal troughs he could survive out here.

The other boy knocks him again. This time the younger one's camera has become wedged between their hips. He had been given the camera for his birthday a few weeks before. He has taken one roll of film already. On the roll in the camera there is just one photograph. The camera was his mother's idea. His father said it was too much and he was too young, but his mother bought it anyway. Her boy seemed to have a talent for it and she wanted to do this for him, wanted also to have this to do with him. He was still her boy. The other two were rapidly approaching their teenage years.

The photograph is of a dog. The boys had discovered it

lying in the road outside their house the day before. Being boys, they poked at it with sticks, even poked its eye as a dare. The youngest did not like this, but he went along with it. He was with his brothers and he didn't want to play alone. He did not take the photograph. It was taken by the middle child, the one sitting next to him now. In fact, it was only this morning, when he checked the camera, that he realised a photo had been taken.

He reaches back for the camera, still not drawing his head in. As he moves it onto his lap, a piece of paper that had been there is lifted up. He tries to grab it before it flies out of the window, but it is gone. It is the scorecard he had filled out from a game of cricket they had been to the day before yesterday. He watches as it is lifted up by the breeze, floating, buffeted, and then comes to rest in the middle of the road.

He closes his eyes now. He can imagine the boy in the field having seen this. The boy would come over, climb the fence, pick up the piece of paper and place it in his pocket. He would keep it safe, put it under his head at night so it would never be lost again.

Before they reach their cottage, they park their car at the side of the road in a mountain pass. There are pools in the valley.

They pick their way through gorse on the slope of the mountain. They move slowly and from a distance seem not to move at all. But the bush sways as they sink through it, like ripples on a pond. They have their arms up, over the surface of the scrub. Only their tops are visible: arms, torsos, heads, drifting to the valley floor. Silt through water.

The father leads the way, a child behind him, his eldest son, followed by the second child. They push the shrubs aside. Their skin, though it cannot be seen from here, is scratched. White on brown. There is a widening gap between the first three and the last two. At the rear, the third child, the youngest, is a few paces behind his mother. Only the top of his head is visible, the head that had been sticking out of the car window an hour before. The thorns of the bush are level with the eyes of the child.

There is no sound. Or, there is the sound made when you put your ear to a shell, a sound that makes you want to put your finger in your ear, let the water out and listen again.

Behind the third child, the broken twigs and leaves of the path they have forged. It leads up the slope, winding along the contours of the mountain and ends at a road, which cuts through the rock and leads, in one direction, to cities, airports, flights away from here. In the other direction, the tarmac grows whiter until it is the colour of the sand that surrounds it and is lost altogether in the paleness of the interminable desert.

The father carries a basket. He holds this in front of him, clearing the branches. The boy behind him has to hold up his arms and catch the branches as they fly back. His face jerks from side to side as he does this. It is a game.

Sweat on the father's face, not the boy's. He does not drop back. He does not give a step. He is twelve. Making his mark. I can do anything, perhaps he thinks. I can fly.

Behind him, his younger brother, his face hidden, shadowed

by the leaves and his own arms held up as well. Over his shoulder a red towel – or brown – it is hard to tell. The picture is faded.

The mother has stopped. She is half-turned towards the youngest child. He is eight. She turns to where he is but cannot see him. Swallowed by the bush. Her lips move. She could be talking to him, shouting at him. John, hurry up. Her lips move, but there is silence.

He has a streak of blood across his face. His mother has not noticed the blood, or if she has, has not mentioned it. He wipes it off. There is not much. What there is sticks to his fingers and he rubs them over a twig. The blood soaks into the bark. He breaks off the twig, crushes it in his hands and feels the splinters cut him. He will not look at her.

She turns away again once she sees him and carries on down the slope. She too is carrying something. An umbrella, perhaps.

They come through the bush, which ends at the rocks on the banks of the river. They come through the bush and out – spat out – onto rocks warmed by the sun. Lizards scatter. The man stands on a rock and looks downstream. From here the river drops rapidly. The eldest child stands nearby, shoulder pointing to his father. The middle boy comes to a halt too. The mother near the father. Then the youngest. He comes through the bush and he sees them lined up there in front of him, sees them on the rocks in the sun, the sun on their backs. He walks between them, picking his way over the rocks. When he's not looking at his feet, he looks at his family. They stand still and silent, looking down the river. He picks his way amongst them, looking up at their faces in shadow.

They have gone. They have gone somewhere and he is left behind. He wants to shout at them, to scream at them. He has felt like this for a while, but does not know why. Not really. There are no words for it now and he will never find words for it. He picks his way between the statues, but does not cry.

Then his father turns to him. Or, his father turns. He says something: 'Here.' Probably that. He shakes out a blanket and sits down. The woman opens the basket, hands him a drink. The eldest boy stays standing on the rock, staring down the river. He turns then and looks back at his parents. The middle child comes and stands next to him.

This boy, the middle child, is hard to see. His face, of all of them, is the most hidden. A sheet of skin drawn over his skull, his mouth an O in the blankness. Do not look directly at him. Look to the side of him. Perhaps then his features will push through the skin and he will come slowly to life.

The other two boys look similar to each other. Save for the gap of four years, they could be twins. They are easier to make out.

The mother sits down. She says something now. The two older boys nod. They all look at the third child and he looks back at his brothers, then at his parents. He looks between them. The elder two set off. His mother waves. At least, her hand moves. The fingers go under the wrist, flick out again. The youngest turns away and begins to follow the others. They are disappearing over the ridge and he runs to catch up.

The three climb down rocks, slip over moss, step around puddles. The youngest drops further and further back, like before. He walks into things, slips, as if he cannot see where he is going. But he does not stop.

They follow the river some way below them now, looking for a way down. They go off the main path. The third child hangs back. It is steep and the rocks are loose beneath his feet.

His feet slip and his face grazes against the rock. He calls out. The eldest boy comes back, but then he goes and the youngest gets up and follows. Barely a mark on him. Not yet. That comes later. Not much later. Just a few seconds.

He follows, but thinks about turning back now. He stands there in the path. He breathes in and out rapidly, his fingers curled into his palms. He opens his mouth to shout and he does, but it cannot be heard. There is no sound that escapes the weight of the mountain, the rocks, the river.

He looks behind him and in front. He can see no one, can hear no one. The ticking of the bush around him like a clock, the heat of it, sweat beginning to seep through his shirt. He starts to turn back, the way he has come. He changes his mind. He begins to walk, then run downhill. It is steep, the stones are loose.

There is a splash. And then another. His brothers are in the water.

He hears something else too before the splash. What that is he cannot yet name.

He hears this. He rolls over, for he is on the ground again, and looks up at the sun. He keeps his eyes open. It hurts. It hurts to do this, but he does it anyway.

After some time – he does not know how long – he peers over the edge at the pool below. He is blinded, but his vision begins to clear. The pool is half in sunlight, half in the shade thrown by the mountain. The water is brown. Clear, but brown. Mountain water leaching the rocks, the plants.

He sees his two brothers in the pool. The water ripples around them. They're half in the sun, half out. They lie on their bellies, backs to the sun, bobbed gently by the water. They are playing a game, pretending to be dead. He says their names over in his head. Paul, Peter.

He wants to go down there, to be with them. But it is too far, too far for a boy of eight.

The parents sit in the sun. They are laughing. The father has his shirt off. He leans over to kiss his wife, his fingertips on her cheek. Then, for a reason that cannot be understood, the smiles are gone. Perhaps they hear something, or sense it. They stand up as one. They are frozen, if only for a second. Then the man starts running. He runs through the rocks, through the bush. He throws himself down the mountain and runs – so it seems to the child who watches him go past – right through it. He runs through it to get to his boys and when he sees them he dives into the pool. He dives – there is still no sound – and grabs one of them. He grabs him by the hair and some of it is torn from the scalp and he pulls the boy across the water and holds him by the neck and throws him onto the rocks. Then he is back for the other and his hands thrash about him.

His fingers hook in the mouth of his child and he pulls and he pulls. This one, too, he throws onto the rocks. The boy bounces on the rocks. The man is out of the water too, next to them, and he looks at one and he sees the whites of his eyes and the blood on his skull and he takes the other and puts his mouth to the boy's and his hands on his chest and there is the crack of a rib. He wants to punch the boy's chest, to get the water out, to get all of it out. He does. He pulls his fist back and lets it go. Again and again. The soft pap of the sound. This can be heard. Only this.

The boy's arm rests over his father's leg. Peter's twelve-year-old arm, soft white hairs on brown skin, rests over the man's leg, like it has done many times before. But not like this. Not like this.

He is breathing. It is something.

From a distance, perhaps perched on a rock up the mountain, reaching over into the blue sky, from there one could see a man rocking back and forth. A man sitting on the rocks, a child on his lap. Another child at his feet, skull crushed and neck twisted to the side. A third lying flat against a different rock, making no sound, his face pressed into the rock. A woman standing, her hands to her mouth. She could be calling to them. She could be saying, 'Come and have lunch.' It is impossible to tell she is screaming, making a noise that cuts through all of them, a noise that they hear and do not hear. From this place you would not know anything was wrong at all. Only the swaying, the rocking of the father, his broken child at his feet, another held to his chest, back and forth, back and forth, only this would give you any clue that this scene was anything other than a family enjoying a picnic in the mountains of the Karoo. Only this would tell you that this scene was somehow not right at all.

2

Rachel was twenty-six when they met. She did not want to be there that evening. Too many bankers, she told him later. She only came to meet a friend who worked in the city.

John Hyde saw her from across the bar. He stopped talking to his friends. He was with a woman – he forgot her name soon after – who caught him staring and shook him by the arm. He barely noticed and did not even glance at her as she left.

As she was leaving, the woman caught Rachel with her elbow, spilling her drink. Rachel looked at her friends, then at the woman now walking out of the door, then shrugged. Forgotten. Never one to brood. Still, this was not where she wanted to be. She picked up her coat, spoke in her friend's ear, and started towards the door.

Her friend grabbed her arm, begging her to stay. Rachel sighed and her eyes drifted over the bar, not looking at anyone in particular. They caught his, caught him staring at her. He smiled. She stared back. She put her coat down, but turned away from John.

He went to the bar and then came and stood behind her, champagne and glasses in hand. Rachel's friend saw him before she did and stopped talking. Rachel followed her gaze and turned around. John did not say anything, just held out a glass. He was surprised when she took it, but did not let on. He gave her friend a glass too and poured for Rachel. She held out a hand while he poured. He pretended to concentrate on the champagne but he looked at the hand too – its pale skin, the unvarnished nails. She did not smile. It was as if she was challenging him, as if she scorned him. He felt this too but kept his hand steady. He poured for her friend, placed the bottle on the table and then went back to his friends. He and Rachel had not exchanged a word. When he got back to his circle he could sense her looking at him. He looked back and smiled. Then he turned his back on her.

She liked his arrogance, she told him a few months later. It annoyed her and attracted her at the same time.

It was an act. He had done it before, though he never told her that. He found it worked. It was a means to an end. She came over to him. It was expected.

Yet, when she did approach and he turned and saw her standing there, and the look on her face, biting her lip, everything went quiet for him. She was standing in front of him and he might as well have been in Antarctica. Around them nothing. He stopped pretending then. She could tell by the look in his eyes, that the pretence, the games were gone.

He did not ask her to go home with him that night – a delicacy in himself that surprised him. He walked to the bus stop with her. He stood close to her, the heat of her body, the scent of her hair. He wanted to put his arms around her. He remembers the gooseflesh, the coldness of her arm beneath his hand.

He watched her get on the bus. She went up to the top and sat on the side of the bus closest to the pavement. She held up her hand to the window, a smile on her face.

He, too, was smiling as he sat in the cab on the way home.

The kiss at the bus stop, the touch of their fingertips. If there was a moment to choose, a moment to fix in time, to nail down so that it didn't get away, that would be the moment for him: the moment that would fix all the others.

They married in Richmond in the summer of 2009. She was twenty-nine, he thirty-four. From the reception, across the white tablecloths and lace, the view was of the expanse of Richmond Park and beyond that the Thames. After a honeymoon in Tanzania, they returned to their flat a few miles further downstream in Battersea.

A day in summer, a Sunday, mid-afternoon. She lies naked on the bed, he next to her. He traces a finger down her spine. Her skin glistens in the sunlight from the open window. His finger runs over the faint white hairs in the small of her back. She turns her head to look at him. Her hair is ruffled, her cheeks pink. They lie like that – she on her stomach, he on his side, his arm supporting his head.

She wants to spend a couple of years establishing herself as a journalist before having children. There is time: they are still young. On this Sunday, they are still young.

A year after their wedding, she had a regular column in *The Times* and was receiving more commissions than she could accept. He was proud of her. Her column had a byline photograph. In the photograph she wore half a smile. She looked sad somehow, even with that smile, distant. As if she knew all about you but not enough at the same time. It was how she had looked on the first night they met. He kept a copy of the photograph in his wallet.

He never thought it ironic, never thought why he liked that photograph so much, the one that made her look as if she knew everything about you, when really she knew next to nothing about him.

She told him stories of her childhood in the Chilterns. She told them in such a way that, when he closed his eyes, he could picture it. He could see her running down a hill, over the rabbit warrens and the chalk flint, arms held out to the side. Flying. Her screams and laughter fill the air. Across twenty years he can hear them. They hang in the air. He feels if he moves his fingers through them, they will waft and disappear.

He feels, when she tells him these stories, that he wants them to hang in the air, does not want them to go, does not want to disturb them. If they stay long enough, then perhaps they will become his too, part of his story.

He tells her stories in turn. He feels he has to offer something. But they are not the truth. He says he is an only child and that his parents died when he was in his early twenties. It might as well be the truth, he tells himself. He makes up stories about a childhood in South Africa. He is good at it. Rather, he takes the story of his childhood and leaves out parts of it. In fact, he leaves out most of it.

Rachel feels there is more. She wants to know why there are no photographs of his parents, why no photographs of him as a boy, why he won't take her to Port Elizabeth where he grew up.

She does not believe the excuses – the story of the fire, always coming up with somewhere else to go on holiday – and feels something is wrong. In fact, she will realise later, it frightens her. Not enough for her to stop loving him, not enough for her to leave, but a little. She has looked him up on the internet of course, but there was not much there and all of it about his career in the city. There is more she could do. She could hire a detective or pay a company that does family trees to research his. But she has promised herself she will wait, will wait for him to tell her.

The first letter arrived on a Saturday morning in March 2011. John went downstairs to get the post, but he did not see it until he was back in the flat, flicking through the envelopes. He stood in the corridor and opened it because she was still getting ready.

It had been snowing. The snow fell late that year. They were about to go to Battersea Park for a walk. The sun was out and it streamed through the window and into the hall. He opened the letter and he stood there in the hall for some time, staring at it. It was a matter of a few lines, but it took a long time before he could take his eyes off it.

He heard Rachel coming out of the bathroom and put the letter in his pocket before she could see it. She came up to him, placed her hand on his arm, and up on tiptoes kissed him. 'Ready?' She smiled up at him. He wanted her then, wanted to be with her, though deep down he knew it was not sex he really wanted. He put his fingers into the top of her jeans and pulled her towards him, put his arms around her and one hand on the top of her leg.

'Let's go back to bed.'

'No, silly. Snowmen.' She laughed and ran through the door, leaving him to lock up.

There was no jump in his heart, no catching of breath when he read the letter. Perhaps some part of him had been expecting it. He read it, but still it did not break down the façade he had built up over the eighteen years since he had left South Africa, and had been building for years before. Not immediately. He did not notice that that was the start of it. He did not show Rachel the letter, not then and not later. Though he did not react to it, he knew it was not for her. Not for her eyes.

It could have changed things if he had, could have changed everything that was to follow.

He had almost forgotten his brother. Or, he had almost managed to stop thinking about his brother.

They throw snowballs at each other. He runs towards her, through her attack, and grabs her around the waist. They fall to the ground, laughing, and lie side by side for a few minutes.

Then he gets to his feet and holds out a hand to her. As he leans down, at the edge of his vision, he sees a man watching them. When Rachel takes his arms and he bends a little further, he loses sight of him. And when he looks again, the man is gone. He is quiet as they walk home. But she is too, and does not notice his silence. She is thinking about something else. About the pill she has not taken that morning. She must remember to take it. It is not yet the time. Soon, but not now.

He forgets the man in the distance. Briefly, he wonders if he made him up, imagined him.

He sees him again, months later. Through the window of their flat, John sees a man standing in Battersea Park amidst the trees that line Albert Bridge Road. He does not see him clearly. The rain on the window, the dark. Only the wind moving the branches of the trees and the light from the streetlamps on the man's face, allow him to see him at all. John stands behind the window in the dark of the room and looks across the street and into the park. When the light comes on him he can see that the man is not looking at him. He looks instead at the window two along, the room in which Rachel is watching television.

She comes into the room now, though, and sees John at the window.

John tracks the man's head moving as it follows her. He still cannot see his face.

'What are you looking at?'

'Peeping Tom.'

She comes towards him, trying to see out of the window,

but he stops her and puts his hand on her arm. She is surprised by the force of it, the look on his face. He is too.

'I'm sure it's nothing, John, just some homeless person. Leave it. If he comes back you can call the police.'

When he looks again later that night, he does not see him.

He almost forgets about the man again. He and Rachel talk about coming off the pill. She is happy. She curls into him. He likes sitting like that. She is small and fits into the crook of his arm. His hand rests on her thigh, her hand on top of his. He folds her into him. He is happy too. He tells himself he is happy. He talks about wanting to have children. He does not think about family. The thought of it would frighten him too much. It is normal, this feeling, he tells himself.

When they sit there on the couch, she says to him, 'If we have a child I would like to name him or her after your parents.'

He looks away from her. He tries to maintain his smile but he feels it going.

'Of course.' He can make something up. There is time. He can lie. 'Of course.'

He thinks about these words. He finds them inadequate. He glances at her quickly and catches her looking at him. He knows what the expression means. He gets up and goes over to the window.

He jumps, visibly he thinks, when he sees the man. Rachel gets up and starts to come over.

He turns to her and holds out his arms. He talks, says the

first thing that comes into his head. 'Peter. They would have liked that.' He takes hold of her and draws her in close. His hands are gripping her arms. When she is close to him and cannot see his face, he closes his eyes and softly shakes his head. He did not mean to say that name. Not that name out of all those he could have said.

He cannot keep it up any more. He has to move away. He goes out of the room and leaves her in the middle of it.

She looks after him, then walks over to the window and looks down at the trees in the park. She sees nothing.

The man starts coming every night. John tries to keep it from his wife. At first he succeeds. He walks past the window and glances at the trees. Sometimes he will see him, sometimes not. He does this several times a night.

Rachel notices. She asks him what he is doing. John says it is nothing, that he is just looking at the view, but he knows she knows it is not true. It is a dance they come to share.

She asks him if he thinks someone is watching them. She wants to call the police. John does not want that. He says it is nothing. He cannot say more than that, cannot give an explanation. He tries, he does try. He finds himself standing at the window, but instead of staring out of it he is lost in thought, trying to think of what to say to her, what she would believe. But he cannot think of anything, and he turns and sees her staring at him and of course he cannot say anything then. He just smiles and walks off.

She has not felt like this before. Though she sensed there

were secrets, they have always been in the background, not, somehow, part of the here and now. But this feeling, it is like she sees something approaching in the distance, a faded image of a thing. She looks at their wedding picture. In the background a darkened smudge. It was not there before. It grows bigger every day.

That evening she finds him and tells him she wants to know what is going on, and if he will not call the police next time then she will. He stops looking then. At least, he stops looking while she is awake.

He waits until she is asleep, listening to her breathing. Then he gets out of bed. He stands in the window and looks out and watches the man watching him.

Of course he recognises him now. He has not yet seen his face completely. But, even when you have not seen him for eighteen years, it is hard not to recognise your brother, especially when you look almost identical.

Peter Hyde comes every night. John stands at his window and sees him, sees his shadow beneath the trees, sees his brother watching the flat.

Once, John runs out of the flat. He tries to be as quiet as possible, but he hurries, knowing that if he cannot be seen at the window his brother might go.

He gets outside but Peter is no longer there. John looks behind the trees, walks up and down the path, but nothing.

He looks up at the flat and there she is: Rachel, framed in the window. The light is behind her so he cannot see her face. He does not know if she can see him. He sees her head moving from side to side, as if searching, scanning the trees. She pulls back from the window and disappears.

He waits, still looking up at the window. He knows he has failed her. It does not surprise him. He should have realised before that what they had was a story, a fiction built on lies.

'What were you doing?' she asks when he comes back.

'Fresh air.'

She says no more. She lets it go. He sees a look on her face, though. So much in that look.

Later that week he is working in his study. She, he thinks, is in the lounge. He can hear the television. It is late and has been dark for an hour. He leans back in his chair, then stands up, turns off the lamp and looks out of the window. He can see nothing.

He goes through to the lounge. She is not there. He calls for her but there is no reply. He goes into each room now, almost running into the last one. She is not in the flat.

In the lounge he looks through the window, cups his hands against the pane. He scans the trees below him. He goes to turn out the light and comes back to the window. As his eyes adjust to the dark, he sees a flash of red in the trees. He tenses. There again, an arm, a leg, the flash of a red coat – hers. And then, right behind it and to the left, in the shadows, a darker shape. He runs out of the flat and across the road and into the park. He stops near where he saw the coat and scans the trees. Nothing. He crouches on his haunches and looks through the hedge. He walks around it and onto the road running through the park. There is no one on it. The road seems to glow as if lit from beneath. He turns. He can hear his own feet on the tarmac. Silence. He is struck by this. There is never silence in London. Even in the quietest moments, the faint hum of life being lived elsewhere. It is as if time has stopped. He closes his eyes. He tries to be calm, breathes in and out. It doesn't work. In his stomach a feeling, a sense he is being watched, a sense there are others who know everything about him, do not like what they see, and are watching what he does next.

He opens the door to the flat. She is there in the hallway. The red coat is on top of the others on the coat rack.

'Where have you been?'

'Out. Did you not hear me? I told you I was going for a walk.'

He hesitates. 'Who were you with?'

'What do you mean? I was alone.'

She walks into the bedroom and he follows.

'I saw someone.'

She does not turn around.

'Did you hear me?'

'Yes, John, I heard you. You said you saw someone. What did you see, John, what did you see?' She sounds tired, he thinks. He knows he cannot blame her, though he knows too he cannot stop.

She begins to take off her top. He watches her from the doorway. 'When are you going to tell me what's going on, John? This is not normal behaviour. This is me. You can tell me anything.'

He listens to her say this. He can hear the words. He knows their meaning. But he cannot speak.

She stands there in her bra, facing away from him, and he goes up to her. He puts his hands around her belly. She tenses beneath him. He can feel this. He leaves his hands where they are. She turns out of his grip, turns half towards him. 'It's late.'

'That's not what I meant.'

She does not reply but goes into the bathroom. He leaves the room then.

Later he comes and stands in the doorway and watches her sleeping. She is on her side of the bed, on the edge, turned towards the outside of the bed. She looks younger like this. Younger than when they first met.

He looks in the morning before he goes to work. There is a broken branch where he thought he saw the man. He wonders, briefly, if he saw him at all, not just last night but every night. He wonders if he has not imagined the whole thing.

And for three days he does not see him.

Then, it is a Friday in late August. The markets are quiet. It is a sunny day. He leaves the bank early and the cab driver drops him at the entrance to Battersea Park. He has not called Rachel. He wants to surprise her. There is a part of him, and for now this part feels as if it is winning, that thinks they can put this behind them, that thinks he, John, can forget what he saw, both over the last couple of weeks and twenty-eight years ago in those mountains on the edge of the Karoo.

John walks down the road through the middle of the park,

past the bandstand and out through the gate on the other side. He goes up to the flat and calls for Rachel. There is no reply. He walks into the study and the main bedroom. The bed is made. The sun shines in through the open window and onto the bed. He sits down there in the warmth. It feels strange being at home this early on a weekday, as if something is wrong.

He calls her mobile but there is no answer. He is about to send a text when he remembers she told him she would be spending the day writing in the park. There is a café in the park where she would sit for hours at one of the tables under a giant oak tree.

He takes his jacket off, lays it on the bed, rolls up his sleeves. He goes out into the park to find her.

John does find her. He approaches the café from the side next to a lake and there she is, where she usually sits. She is facing him but does not see him. He is still some way off. She has her laptop open in front of her, but is talking to someone. A man. He has his back to John and he cannot see his face. He does not need to see it.

He stands still. Children ride their bikes past him, mothers push buggies. They look at him. He does not notice. The day has grown cold.

Peter gets up. John notices something on the table next to Rachel. It looks like a piece of paper. She is staring at it.

John moves forward and holds onto the fence that separates the lake from the path.

His brother is walking away. Rachel looks only at the paper. It is an envelope.

John has a choice. He can go to Rachel. He can run up to her and stop her reading the letter. He knows it is a letter. He knows it is not something she should read.

Or, he could go after his brother. He has a sense that, if he does not do this now, he will never catch him, will never be able to talk to him again. And though he does not believe it is for him to make this move, given the events of twenty-eight years ago, something still compels him. He watches Peter's back disappear down the path into the trees.

He is frozen.

Then Rachel makes up his mind for him. She gets up and takes the letter. She does not open the envelope but carries it in her hand as she leaves the café.

He cannot let it out of his sight.

He follows her home. She does not see him. When she disappears into their building, he panics and runs across the road. A car hoots at him. He bursts into the flat a few seconds after her.

She stands in the hallway. The light from the window at the far end floods in and catches her. He is blinded. She stands there, hands at her sides.

'It's for you.' She hands him the letter.

He takes it, feels the weight of it.

'He looks so much like you.' The words are unreal to him, so soft. With the noise in his ears he barely hears them.

A picture comes to his mind. He does not know why he thinks of this, why he cannot focus on what is happening in front of him. He hates himself for it. He is standing in the middle of a frozen lake in Siberia. It is silent. There is no wind. He has never experienced silence like this before. He opens his mouth to speak and his breath freezes as it comes out of his chest. It is so quiet he can hear the tinkling of his frozen breath as it falls to the ground.

She breaks the silence. 'I miss you.'

He looks at her, still unable to speak.

'I can't do this any more, John. I love you but this is not how it is supposed to be. I am leaving.'

He goes up to her then, the letter still in his hand. He can feel she has not opened it. He puts his arm around her. Still he cannot speak, his breath frozen inside him. He holds her, but he cannot put both his arms around her because the letter is in one hand and he knows he should put it down and hold her properly, do this for her at least, but he cannot and she is lifeless in front of him, cold in his half embrace.

3

I am standing at Peter's grave after his funeral. There is a line of blue gum trees in front of me. They are smaller and thinner than I remember.

The mourners are gone. I do not mean mourners. There was me, a priest and a few people from the funeral home. That was it. It seems Peter did not have many friends, though admittedly I did not put up a death notice and did not go out of my way to find people who knew him. There is something private about this, something that is between me and him. It may be selfish but selfishness is not what matters at this point.

I phoned the police from Heathrow to tell them this was going to happen. They said they would send a car to the house to check on him. I did not hear back. I tried again from the airport in Johannesburg. The person I spoke to was not aware of my earlier call but promised to call me back with information. By the time I got to Port Elizabeth my phone was dead and I had forgotten my charger. I could have used a payphone, but it would not have made any difference and I wanted to get to the house as soon as possible.

The police were too late.

I did all I could. I followed him out here from London, called the police, twice, rushed off to the house I hadn't seen in eighteen years. I did what I could.

The plots are laid out in front of me. My mother next to Paul. Next to her my father. My parents' names. I stare at the words. Neil. Sarah. They could be strangers. They could be anyone. Peter is laid on Paul's left. It is good they are together, in spite of what happened. It was an accident. Peter could not have meant that to happen, could not have meant to push him; he would just have intended to give him a little fright. They were boys after all.

I wish I had brought something – for all of them. Flowers, anything. I get to my hands and knees. I begin pulling up the weeds on their graves, one by one. The ground is hard. I uncover glass, bits of crockery. I scrape at the sand and the weeds with my bare hands and it takes ages to clear it and by the end the tips of my fingers are bleeding. The graves are bare, though clean. It is something.

I struggle to think of these people as family. Paul and my mother died many years ago, my father when I was in my early twenties, and I had not spoken to Peter for eighteen years, though I did see him briefly in London just days ago. That I saw him there after all this time makes this seem unreal. In fact, if he came up behind me now and tapped me on the shoulder, I might not be very surprised.

I will come back here. Before I return to London, I will bring flowers. It is a small thing to do.

I have the key to the house in my pocket. I have not been back since that first day. Perhaps if I had been back, I would have looked up friends of his, invited them to the funeral. No doubt there is an address book somewhere. But I did not. It is done.

Innisfree – that's what my father called the house. It was a joke. It must have been a joke. No verdant utopia. Rather a pile of red bricks set in soil so grey, so dry, it runs through your fingers like sand in an hourglass.

There was no jolt, no pang of longing when I saw the house for the first time. It was like looking at any other house. For a few seconds in fact, I wondered if I had ever lived there, if indeed this was a different house and any recognition merely a product of my imagination.

I am in no hurry to get back to the house. I do not drive straight there and instead take a detour. From my hotel room, where I've been staying since arriving in Port Elizabeth, I could see St George's Park which I remember from my childhood. I drive there, park the car and walk up to the gates of the cricket ground.

There was a day with Dad, Paul and Peter. We went to watch a game of cricket. I do not remember who was playing. Eastern Province, most likely, but I do not remember their opponents.

I was keeping score. I used to love doing that. We went

35

often and I kept all the scorecards, though, now I think about it, that one was lost a few days later.

There was a cup of Coca-Cola filled with ice. I placed it between my feet so I could mark a run with one hand, holding the scorecard on my lap with the other. I can see the shoes on either side of me – now, I mean. I can see them as if it is happening now. It is clear. Not shoes, sandals. I see the dust too, a splash where my own drink has spilled. The foot to my right, Paul's, is brown, burnt by the sun. Half of the nail is missing: a bicycle accident. I had forgotten that. It is strange how these things come back, not just this memory but other things too. Other things I have forgotten or thought I had forgotten.

A wicket falls, and Dad, Peter and Paul jump up and I do too, and as I do, I kick the cup and it falls onto the seat of the person in front. He turns around. Dad has to apologise. He makes me apologise too. I remember the blood in my cheeks, the prickles at the back of my neck. Peter pushes me and sniggers.

I realise this day would have been just before Paul died. It was the last time the four of us were on our own – the men of the family. Three men, one boy, it felt at that moment.

I close my eyes to try and recapture the vision of the foot. I watch me as a boy sit down and look to the right, but the foot has gone. I have lost sight of Paul. I can no longer see him, no longer conjure him up.

There was a time I could conjure him up easily. I remember a dream I had shortly after he died. It's funny how I struggle to remember many real events from that time, but a dream is still vivid.

I was lying in bed. It was one of those dreams in which you think you are awake but cannot be. I was lying in bed and he came into the room. It was dark, but I knew it was him as soon as he came through the door. I lay there and he came up to me and stood right next to me. I could have touched him. His right side was facing me so I could not see the crushed half of his skull. But I knew it was there.

I was ill, I remember now – feverish. A dog had bitten me a few days before. Just a scratch, I think. Perhaps it was not that.

He looked at me and in the dark I could see there was no expression on his face. It was blank.

He was beautiful. South Africa in the 1980s. You tried to be men but that was the word that came to me: beautiful, this dead boy. My brother, the boy I wanted to play with, the boy I wanted to be. I almost cried.

He stood there looking and after some time I wanted him to go, I did not want to look at him any more, did not want him to look at me and remind me he was dead. I pushed the blankets off and put my feet on the carpet and stood up. He was right in front of me. I could smell him. The smell of water. I tried not to look at him.

I shuffled to the right. He followed. Then to the left. He kept pace with me. I tried to trick him by moving one way and then rapidly in the other, but I could not get rid of him. He penned me in. I remember this dance. I remember it going on for the whole night. It seemed like an eternity.

I was eight. Having suffered the trauma of losing a brother in an accident I witnessed, it is no wonder I had nightmares.

Back in the car I head down a road called Park Lane. It takes me back momentarily to London, to my life there. I spent a lot of time on Park Lane and in the hotels there. A different world. The person who did that, who sat through those meetings, seems a stranger to me.

Port Elizabeth is a grey city. Coming back was not what I expected. There are parts I don't recognise, but mostly it is as if I have never left. There are bumps in the road I feel I remember. Trees that must have grown but look the same. The same restaurants – or, they look the same. Over everything a film of dust. I think that if I could scrub it off, the city would match what I remember from my childhood: the sparkle, the newness that I felt for much of the time, until Paul's death cast a shade over it.

In the streets and the shops, the hotel, the few restaurants I have been into, there are only strangers. I thought maybe I would recognise one or two people from my teenage years. But either they have left or changed so much I cannot recognise them. I do not belong here any more in this familiar city filled with strangers. The echo of home.

I have been picked up and placed in another time.

I look in the rearview mirror. There are no cars in the road. There are some parked at the side, but nothing moves. Everyone is at home asleep in front of the television on this Sunday afternoon. I have grown used to London. It is never quiet there. Never quiet enough to lose yourself in your thoughts.

This emptiness was something I noticed when I arrived. Walking through the airport, my footsteps echoed in the halls. There was no traffic on the roads. The houses next to Peter's seem empty. The first house is an old bungalow and it has its windows boarded up. The house on the other side looks empty too, and I cannot see the house opposite from the road.

Perhaps if I stay, I will come to feel differently, get to know this place again, love it even. But there is no chance of that. I will go back to London – though, it is true, I have somewhat burnt my bridges there. My wife has left me. I will be fired from my job very soon, if it hasn't happened already, as I have not told them why I am not at work. Still, I can find another job and it is not like I need the money anytime soon.

I smell the tarmac. Another thing that is the same. The smell of the place.

I drive past my old school. When I get close, I look over at the buildings across fields. They are cream and brown, smaller than I remember. There is an area at the side. It is covered in tar now. I played there during breaks: with marbles, spinning tops. It was covered in gravel and red dirt. I remember the dust on my black shoes. I drew lines in the dirt on them. The shine beneath the dust. I stop the car and get out.

I am surprised I know the way so well, the way we used to drive, the road we turned into to get up to the main road, the Cape Road. I remember, I can picture, my mother behind the steering wheel. Always her. Dad was at work.

The details come back: the dust, the roads, the lines on her face.

It was always my mother driving. This was the same after it happened too. After Paul died, it was the same. Always my mother, as if nothing had happened – for a while at least.

I would watch her. When it was my turn in the front seat, I would watch the bones of her fingers around the steering wheel, her lips held tight together. She was not someone who did this as a matter of course, not an ungenerous woman, but she was a very careful driver.

I sometimes thought she was angry with us, with me, for some reason. Perhaps this was only after Paul died. She seemed angry all the time. I suspect this was just a child's imagination, however. Sad, yes. She would not have been angry with me.

In this vision, if that's what to call it, I turn my head and see two other children in the back of the car. They look at me. They have smiles – no, I will call them smirks – on their faces. They have been whispering to each other. Somehow I know it is about me. I turn slowly back and face the road again.

A car turns the corner further down the road. For a time it is our car. It is our car and I have been left behind at school. I think that if I run fast enough I could catch it at the next light, catch it and grab the handle and tug at it and they would let me in.

This place has had a strange effect on me. Memories have returned. That is not unexpected of course, but it is the way they return. I see things and sometimes wonder if they are real. I see people and wonder if they are in fact here in front of me, or if they are ghosts, figments of my imagination. I would reach out and touch them but I doubt that would sit well with them if indeed they are real.

I am sure this feeling will pass. I know what causes it. Half a life lived here, half a life somewhere else, a return, and with the return the awakenings of a time past. It is like jumping into a mountain pool. The silt is disturbed but it will settle again soon enough and it will be like nothing ever happened.

A flower from a jacaranda tree falls on my arm. I pick it off and crush it between my fingers.

It is darker now. A few houses have lights on. As I walk past one on my way back to the car, a dog rushes up, barking. There is a fence and the dog hurls itself against it but cannot get through. Something stirs in me at the sight of this animal. I stand and watch as it grows more frantic. A light comes on at the side of the house and I walk away quickly.

Back in the car, I come to a point where the road forks and I turn left. The houses here are set further back from the road. There are no streetlights any more.

I open the windows as I drive. I can see leaves framed against a black sky. The trees smell like dust. A smell of a home I once had but which now I don't know and which does not know me.

It hit me as I stepped off the plane – the smell of the place. I stopped at the top of the stairs until the person behind me asked me to move.

At the airport I gave them my British passport. My South African one has long since expired and I have never wanted to renew it. It felt like I was doing something wrong. I was expecting the woman who looked at my passport to take it with her, walk out of the booth and up to her supervisor. She would point and they would both stare. The exile returns. Who does he think he is?

Outside the gate to the house, I park the car, get out and look down the drive at the house. I close my eyes and remember the rooms: the hall, the lounge, dining room, study. Upstairs, too. I focus on one room: the bedroom that leads to the attic. The details are clear: concrete floor, a dark patch in one area, wooden beams, fresh splinters on one.

The lights are off.

I do not go in immediately. The keys are in my pocket and I feel the shape of them. I look around me. There is no one else here, no one on the road. From here I cannot even see a neighbour's house, let alone someone inside. I do not feel alone, though. Possibly, here, I never could. I find myself wishing I did feel alone.

I sit against a tree for a time, not waiting for anything in particular, just waiting. My hands rest on leaves and I burrow into them a short way. I would like to go further in, pull a blanket of them over me. I picture myself digging through the leaves, sand, rocks, slowly burrowing my way towards the house. If I made enough tunnels, dug them close enough to the surface, then perhaps cracks would begin to appear in the walls of the house and the roof and then the whole thing would collapse. I, somehow not crushed by the weight of it, trapped nonetheless by the walls, buried deep in soil.

I could leave. I wonder why I don't. What is there for me here? What is this plan that says I have to spend time here? In truth I do not know. If I am honest, I do not know what I want to accomplish. Peter wrote a letter. In it, the product of a brain showing the first signs of a tumour, he made some accusations. Not accusations, suggestions. They rankle. By being here, I feel, I can put things right again, reorder events the way they should be, the way they have been.

Twenty-eight years since Paul died. Can we be certain of events that far in the past? Our minds change things, alter the sequence, alter intent, and when, as was the case with Peter, a mind is riddled with cancer, then what indeed are the chances? It might as well all be make-believe.

The letter from Peter, the things he wrote – I attribute it all to cancer. But that is not all. The lies and insinuations no doubt prompted by his guilt over what happened, over what he did.

I know this is the reason for me staying a little longer, this wanting to put things right again. I am not blind to this. I want to put it behind me, as I did once before.

I look up at the sky. Still no stars. There is the noise of an owl, and crickets, always the crickets.

4

It is dawn when I wake. I have slept more soundly than I did in the hotel. There is a spider on my leg. I kick it off and wipe my face in case there are more. I feel dirt wiped onto my face, and dampness. I grit my teeth and there is dirt in them too, as if I have spent the night underground.

The damp is from mist that descended in the night. It is thick and I cannot see the house.

I get up, piss against a tree. My head hurts, my neck too.

I walk down the road to the gate. When I begin to see the shape of the house, I stop. It seems lighter like this. As if I could walk up to the house and then straight through it. Or, wave my arm and watch it break and curl away, like smoke. I hold my breath as if even that could make it disappear.

I stand in the hall. All is quiet. I draw in a breath and hold it. Silence. The house smells closed up. Something died in here, I find myself thinking.

I listen. I realise I am listening for Peter.

I take it in this time, the house I mean, look around me

properly. Here in the hallway the tiles are different. The carpets are probably different too, but they are the same colour as I remember from my childhood. In front of me, in the lounge, is a sideboard. My father kept liqueurs there. I stare at it. He appears before me, as if real: my father. He is dressed in shorts and a collared shirt. This is Port Elizabeth in the early 1980s. He comes into the lounge, a grin on his face. Though I cannot hear anything, there is the sense that someone is talking to him. A joke. He goes up to the sideboard and kneels and I see his bald spot that we used to tease him about before Paul died, and I see him open the cupboard and take out a bottle and two glasses. He opens his mouth and shouts something, but there is still no sound. He laughs, but again nothing.

Then he stops, as if he has heard something. An intruder. He turns his face towards me, half turns. My heart stops. He does not see me. Of course he does not see me. But he is looking right at me. I cannot help looking behind me to see if there is someone there, but it is me he is looking at. There is still a grin on his face, but it starts to fade, to disappear and his shoulders slump as if under an unbearable weight.

I shake my head to get rid of this thought, or vision, whatever it should be called. Walking into a place like this, the house in which you grew up, is bound to have a strange effect, bound to awaken memories or conjure visions. I feel I can imagine them here. My family. Smell their scent. As if they have just left the room I enter.

I walk through the house and open windows. I need to get the air in.

I sniff the damp air. Maybe the smell comes from out there, not the house itself but that which surrounds it.

The kitchen is as I remember. The tiles are the same. There are still flowers on them in places where they haven't been worn away. The cupboards, too, are exactly the same. For a moment I wonder if they are in fact the same or whether my mind is playing tricks on me. Perhaps I have forgotten everything, and am fooling myself that I remember. Perhaps the tiles were replaced soon after I left with a similar pattern, and then perhaps once or twice more, each pattern resembling the one before. The last pattern is definitely not the first, but able to pass for the first because of the gap of twenty years. Somehow the weight of change eliminates the difference from the first.

In the lounge there is a photograph on the table, covered in dust. I pick it up. Three boys, two with their arms around one another. I wipe away some of the dust. On the back are the names Peter, Paul and John, and a date, 11 December 1983. As if the names and the date could be forgotten.

Beneath this photograph is another. A boy, his back to the camera, sits on the ground clasping his legs to him. He is in a forest, or at least in the bush. We do not have forest here.

It is Peter. I took the photograph.

I go upstairs, open more windows. I stop at the entrance to the main bedroom. The bed is unmade. I wonder at this. The rest of the house is neat, prepared. Why wouldn't he have made the bed? He knew I was coming, would have guessed I would come. That, surely, was the point of the letter: to goad me into flying out here after him.

I pull the sheets off and hold them up. They are yellow where he has laid on them. I sniff. They smell of a person, a man. I don't know what I expect. To recognise the smell?

I detect a faint warmth on the sheets. The sun slants across the bed.

There are no beds in the other rooms. The first room down the corridor was Paul's. There are some cupboards built in, but otherwise the room is empty. The next one belonged to me. The furniture is the same as I remember: white cupboards, a desk under the window. I feel nothing, though. I cannot see myself in here.

I walk out and turn to go further down the corridor, but I stop. Something makes me turn around. I am not sure what exactly. I step back into Paul's room. It is empty. There is a noise, though. Rather, not a noise, a sudden absence of noise. Like my eardrum has stopped working. It lasts just a moment.

I stare out of the window which looks out over the driveway, briefly picturing Peter returning, but of course there is nothing out there.

I do not go into the last bedroom: Peter's room as a boy. I stand outside it, where I can see the door to the attic room. There are bolts on it, one of which has been drawn. The police appear to have cleaned up well after themselves.

To my left, a window. The mist has not burnt off yet. It is like I am at the top of a mountain looking into cloud. And then, through the mist, a brighter spot, a white disc.

In the lounge I sit in the chair and pick up the phone. There is no dialling tone. The bills have not been paid, I assume.

I do not know Rachel's number anyway. I have never had to remember it since it was in my mobile. I could buy a charger for it, but I think it is better if I do not call.

I hear a knock on the front door. At least I think I hear it. I may have been asleep and dreaming. It is like I hear it some time after it has happened. I turn my head towards the door and listen. I hear nothing further, but I get up and go to the door. As I pass the second lounge, I see a shadow on the floor, something standing in front of the window, unmoving. I can see the shape of the head, the rest of it formless. I stop, then move closer. As I step into the room, a cloud, or the last of the mist, moves across the window and the shadow vanishes. I peer around the door. Nothing. There is also nowhere anyone could have gone. The windows are still open, but there are bars across them. There are two marks where someone could have been standing, but they are more likely just scuff marks. I stand on top of them. The sun casts my shadow, nothing else. I step to one side, hear my feet move on the carpet. The shadow stays where it is. Not a shadow at all: the light from the sun picking out an old stain. I open the front door but there is no one there either.

I spend the night on the couch. I have washed and hung out the bed sheets but they are not dry yet. The house is quiet. I hear only the occasional tick. I lie on the couch and watch the moonlight as it shifts across the ceiling.

Just before dawn, I go out of the house and into the garden. There is no mist today. The last of the stars are in the sky, and the wind, for once, is still, quiet.

Later I drive to a shopping centre and go into a hardware store. I buy tins of paint, brushes, white spirits, cloths, dust sheets, a sander.

I take my purchases out to the car and pile them in the boot. I have no firm plan yet, which is unlike me, beyond staying for a few more days before putting the house on the market. I will use the time to give the place a coat of paint.

I have never been good at DIY, though I think I can manage to tidy the place up a bit, make it more marketable for when the time comes to sell it. From what I can see, it would be hard to give houses away here, though. The bungalow on the left as I look up the road has boards across its windows and the one beyond that has a 'For Sale' sign outside. I have seen no signs of life from the house on the right, though it is more difficult to see from here than the one on the left. There is open land behind Peter's house. It is still scrub. Not much has changed. On the way here I noticed that all the houses are set back from the road. I try to remember if I have ever seen anyone in the gardens, but I cannot.

I call it Peter's house, as if he is still alive. I find it hard to think of it as my house, though legally it is mine now – or will be very soon – and once it was as much mine as it was his. The familiarity of it somehow makes it less possible for me to make it my own. I was a very different person when I lived here, almost a stranger. It is him that should claim it – that boy that I was.

I allow my thoughts to wander. It is years earlier, and I have returned, forgiveness on my mind. Peter and I occupy separate wings. The house is not big enough to have wings but it is not far off. We extend, perhaps rip out the attic room and put in an en suite. We meet local women, marry them. In a year or two, children. We gather in the middle of the house for family meals, Peter and I at opposite ends of the table. Patriarchs. Perhaps we would take holidays in the Karoo. A car trip to Barrydale and the mountain pass and a picnic in the river valley.

Our very own dynasty. A line of Hydes, beginning here, spreading out to populate the world.

In this reverie, I give Peter my face. We always looked alike and I have not seen him up close for many years – not alive anyway.

I feel something: embedded in the fabric of this place, this house, city, country, a past that repels me. At the same time, though, the scent of it, the sense of it floating around me, in the dust on the air, buried in the layers of paint on the walls, it has its hook in me, a fish hook ripping through my gullet. The house pulls me in.

I don't want it – any of it. Did I want reconciliation with Peter by coming out here, by trying to prevent what I saw coming? I have long felt revulsion for him, for what he did, though I know I should not blame him. And, here I lay it out in the open, I do not want to be in the house of a man to whom I have not spoken in eighteen years; I do not want to be reminded of those terrible events when my brother died. Peter drew me here with that letter, with those half-truths, those untruths, and the threat, implied or not.

I am annoyed with myself, I should never have come.

I will go back to London and try to resume my life, with Rachel if she will have me. My brother will be out of my life then, once and for all. It is decided.

I will sort the house out, put it up for sale, and then get back on a plane.

I unroll plastic sheeting on the floor, move furniture away from walls, cover that in plastic too, wash the walls, tape the edges of the windows, remove light fittings, switch and plug covers. It is while doing this that I discover the cameras. Each room has what appears to be a motion-activated camera, installed no doubt for security purposes. I have found no evidence of any other security or recording equipment though and do not give the cameras much thought.

For a week I paint through the day and into the night. Each night I sleep, I imagine, without moving, in the centre of the bed, arms at my sides. I do not shower, do not clean myself at all. I am covered in paint – my hair, even my feet, as I discover when I remove my shoes to go to bed, have paint on them, as if I have somehow unknowingly taken my shoes off in the middle of painting.

I notice, as I go through each room, there are marks on the carpet where furniture has stood. It is as if he had been getting rid of it in preparation for my arrival. Some of it I can even remember. I picture the dining-room table, standing in the middle of the room. Doors leading out onto the patio. Seated at the table are my mother, father, Peter and myself. I have scabs all over me. Week-old cuts and grazes. Paul is not there. My mother scrapes at the food on her plate. Peter stares at me from the opposite end of the table. I do not meet his gaze. It is not an accusatory stare. It is something else. As if he is pleading with me. Perhaps he has asked me to pass the salt. I sense that if I look at him, he will not meet my gaze. My father is looking at both of us as if he thinks there is something between us.

Do I remember this? Or, do I only remember sitting at the table and the rest is made up? Embellished by time and the dislocation I feel being back here.

I have not opened many of the cupboards or drawers that remain – it does not feel right somehow – but when I move an item of furniture I can feel it is empty. He wrote in his letter that he had cleared out most of the contents and he seems to have done a thorough job.

I know there are some items that remain and I will need to clear everything out of course before selling, but first I will paint the whole house: every room except the one under the eaves, the one leading off Peter's old bedroom. There is nothing in there to paint: it is just brick, concrete and raw wood.

I do find something in one of the kitchen cupboards, though. I am looking for a jar in which to wash a paintbrush, and I find a document. A strange place for it but Peter was probably not the most logical man. It is a title deed in Peter's name and the address is the bungalow next door, the one that is boarded up.

I stand at the window that looks out towards the house. Something flaps in the wind and catches my eye. One of the boards that was nailed across the window has come loose, or was always loose, I am not sure. I have not noticed it before. I go outside and walk up to the fence and watch it flapping back and forth.

I go back inside the larger house and have a shower, wash most of the paint off and change into fresh clothes. I am passing the window when I see the board move again. I know it is the wind that moves it, but something makes me go back out to the fence and stand there for a few minutes. Every window I can see, besides the one that caught my eye, is boarded up. The garden is overgrown but sparse at the same time. It does not rain much here. There are trees on the far side of it. They lean to the right, bent by the wind.

I feel, though only briefly, I am being watched. I dismiss it. Sometimes solitude can conjure up ghosts.

I look along the fence, and there, a short distance away, is a gap. The wire is old and here the fence seems to have simply rusted away. Or perhaps, some time ago, it was cut. I step through. There is no grass here, only sand. My feet kick up clouds of it, though I try to move lightly. I walk up to the single-storey building, the walls a dull brown. I walk around it until I reach the window with the broken board. The ground in front of it is undisturbed, as far as I can tell. I peer through the gap. The glass is still in place, though grimy. I rub some of the dirt away and place my forehead against the window, my hands shielding the glare. My eyes take a few seconds to adjust. On the wall opposite me is a painting of a scene in England, where I now call home. At least I imagine it is England: a babbling brook, a green meadow, a water mill. It is out of place here, does not belong. I feel, and I cannot explain this, anger. I think that is the word. I force myself to look away.

The rest of the room is almost empty. There is a dresser along one wall and in the middle of the room a chair on its side.

I walk around the house. At the back is a porch. There are dead cactus plants in pots. Plastic sheeting covers one end of the porch – protection from sun and wind. I imagine an old couple here, their ghosts. They drink tea, eat ginger cake, wear cardigans. Perhaps they talk about their neighbour – the man who lives by himself after his father's death and who never married and never goes out and is a bit strange, but also maybe a bit sad. They do not think that one day he will own their house. I think back and try to picture who lived here when I was young, but I cannot.

There is a sliding door. There are no boards across it. I would be able to see in but for the closed curtains. I pull the door and it begins to open.

We would have known these people, even if just in passing. I do not remember them. I have no recollection of this house at all.

I write 'We.' I have no business writing 'We', I know that.

As I slide the door open, I listen for an alarm, but I do not expect one nor hear one. I reach in and move the curtain aside.

The house smells as if it has been closed for some time. Mouldy. It would take a lot to get rid of this smell. I will not paint this one, I find myself thinking.

The room I step into is a lounge. There is an old chair that faces a television. I sit in the chair and look towards the television. I can see my reflection in it. The arms of the chair are sticky. I get up quickly.

I walk through the rooms. It is smaller than Peter's house. I make this distinction, though this one belongs to him too. The lounge leads into a passageway. Three bedrooms and a bathroom, each empty, open off it. They are dark and I cannot see clearly, but I can see they are empty. Then I go into the dining room, the room with the loose shutter. It is lighter in here but there is not much to see. I take the painting off the wall, lay it face down on the ground and return to the lounge.

I see it then and I wonder why I did not notice sooner. There is a laptop on the floor near the TV. It is plugged in and I can see a light glowing. It is still on. Next to the laptop is a pile of seemingly blank DVDs. One case, though, lies apart from the others and is empty.

I press a key and the TV screen comes to life. The picture in front of me is of Peter. He is frozen in black and white, blurred. His face fills the screen and his eyes appear to be closed. In truth he is unrecognisable but I know it is him. Who else would it be, after all? Besides, this figure looks like me and I know it is not me.

I remember the cameras installed in the house next door.

I play the DVD. Peter springs back to life. I see him walking from room to room. That is all. The DVD is a collection of scenes of Peter doing nothing.

Until the end. He goes into the room in the eaves. There is a camera in that room too. He goes in there and he does not come out. And then I appear. I run into the room after him. On the DVD it is a split second after Peter; in reality it was a full day later. I rewind and watch over and again. But there is nothing else. This is all there is, all that is left of him. I flick through the other discs, but this is the only one out of its wrapper.

The room is silent. Not completely silent; there is a buzzing that comes from the screen. I put my finger in my ear but the sound does not change. Not from the TV or laptop then.

I leave, closing the door behind me. I stand still in the dark for some time. I do not know how long. I stand in the dark and when I do move, my limbs creak as if suddenly I have lost years of my life.

5

I am at the fence walking back to the larger house when I see it. Just a glimpse, fleeting. I am looking elsewhere – at my feet – and I catch it at the edges of my vision: a man disappearing around the side of the house.

The first thing I think is that the hours – for it is hours – I have spent in the dark, watching the DVD, has affected my vision. But that feeling lasts for just a moment.

I run. I run through the gap in the fence and round to the right of the house, the opposite direction to the figure, hoping to intercept him. My route takes me around the pool wall. A mistake. I am out of sight of the house for too long. I have locked it, though, I am certain of that. I emerge onto the lawn at the back of the house but can see no one. I run again, looking inside through the windows. When I get to the front of the house, I have still not caught sight of the intruder. I walk all the way around the house again and through the yard this time. Nothing.

I go into the swimming pool enclosure, opening the gate

in the fence that runs along the side opposite the wall. I have not been in here yet. It has not been kept up. There is a metre of water in the deep end, a few centimetres in the shallow. I cannot see the bottom because of the leaves. I walk around the edge of the pool looking into it. For what, I am not sure. The sludge is undisturbed. In one end a crisp packet, faded by the sun.

I remember this place. Three boys. Long summers. I remember diving in, a towel around my shoulders. We had been watching *Superman*. I dived in on top of Peter as he lay on a lilo. He screamed at me. I remember being shocked at this. I had just been playing a game. It was wrong of him to react like that, even if he had been hurt. He swam off and did not speak to me for hours. In fact, I think the next time was in the car on the way to the Karoo. Our parents asked what was wrong, but neither of us said anything.

I look back at the house and away from the water. I am annoyed I have allowed myself to get sidetracked by a memory.

But whatever it was is gone. I am left feeling unsettled. I will call it unsettled. Whoever it was – not whatever.

What has thrown me most, though, is what I thought when I first saw the person. Peter: I thought it was him. Though I caught only a fleeting glimpse and could not have recognised him, I thought it was Peter.

A few days later I finish painting the house. It looks better. I have not done the best job but it will do. I have painted around the cameras, leaving them in place.

But I have made no move to sell the house or book a flight back to London. I am in the house of the man to blame for the death of my brother and cut out of my life because of it, a man who has also to bear at least some responsibility for what happened after Paul's death: our own estrangement, my mother's growing absences and eventual departure, the silences between the three who remained.

I am here, sitting in the same chairs he sat in, using the same bathroom, sleeping in the same bed. I feel him all around me. It's as if he is seeping into me, this man I could not wait to get away from, whom I have been trying to forget my whole life. I feel as if he is somehow watching me, perhaps because of the cameras I feel peering down at me. I feel him sat in the bungalow before the screen, half a smile on his face, enjoying watching me flounder.

Why? I ask myself. Because I witnessed Paul's death? Because I saw what happened and never told? It is more than that. What he wrote in that letter. He seems to have forgotten what happened, forgotten the truth of those events.

I cannot picture his face. Though I saw it just hours ago, I cannot picture it. When I try there is blankness where his face should be.

Or, I picture my own. I think of this man, for whom I feel only distaste, and instead I see my own face. Despite my inertia, I cannot wait to be rid of this, of all of this.

I resolve to change that and complete the clearing of the house. I have not opened any cupboards, any drawers yet. Though I have been here a few weeks, though I have painted the whole house and moved furniture, I have shied away from opening cupboards and drawers where there might be some reminders of the past.

I sit in the chair in the lounge, facing out to the garden, and I know what I must do, what I have been putting off all these days and weeks. I cannot move, though. It is as if I cannot feel my limbs, or, as if there is something sticking through my chest, through my spine, pinning me here. A needle through a fly.

It is one thing painting the house, quite another going into the heart of it, the guts of it. I begin, though, and start going through the cupboards. There are a few I have opened already: the kitchen, the one in the upstairs corridor where I assumed I would find bed linen. But not many. None in the bedrooms. They are mostly empty. Things may have been stolen of course. There have been plenty of people in the house recently. But I do not think that is the case and I remember again what he said in his letter about leaving only a few things behind.

As I start going through the drawers, I get a strong sense of him. It is like he is here with me, inside the house. Perhaps, I find myself thinking, there is another room, one I have forgotten about, in a corner of the house, where now he stays and watches; his death an elaborate charade, a trick performed with mirrors and lights and cameras.

This thought somehow does not strike me as ludicrous. I keep expecting to see him, keep expecting to be confronted by him as I walk from room to room. A man, flesh and blood. If not here, then in the house next door. I am less familiar with that. Perhaps he bought it and excavated underground, a hideaway unknown to the world. He flits between the two houses, always in the one I am not.

In one of the cupboards there is some linen. In another, empty boxes and magazines dating from five years ago. The cupboards in the main bedroom are the fullest. I pull clothes from them. I hold up a shirt, hold it up first to the light then to me. My size. Most I throw quickly into bags but a few I keep aside. There are no suits, few formal clothes.

From the drawer next to the bed I pull out junk. There are wires, buttons, a few coins, a penknife, a pack of cards. I take the cards out. They are still in the cellophane wrapper. I wonder at this. Did he go out and buy a pack of cards? I wonder who they might have been for, if they were meant for someone else, to be dealt by someone else, to someone else. But never used. I imagine a scene: my brother in the lounge downstairs. Two glasses of wine on a table. The lights turned low. A pack of cards, two hands dealt. On the chair opposite, a woman, her hair shielding her face. She flicks it and I see it is her: Rachel, my wife. I close my eyes and the picture goes.

I am used to those pictures by now. Rachel and Peter: the image of them talking in the café in the park. A period of my life I am trying not to think about. I did not handle it well, lost control. Thinking back, it was as if I was afraid of my brother, though without reason.

I wonder if there is, or was, a woman. I surmise not, given what was implied in the letter he wrote. No children either. But I could be wrong. Perhaps now, at this very moment, a woman is driving from the airport on her way to see him. She has been away for months on an aid mission, working for the Red Cross. She will ring the doorbell, skirts to her ankles, expecting a different man to open the door, not this one, one who looks similar, the same even, but who is very obviously not whom she is here to see. A doppelgänger.

Perhaps she will be holding a child by the hand, a girl with streaky hair and round brown eyes. My niece. My family. The story makes no sense. There is no girl.

In another drawer are more papers and a box closed with an elastic band. I empty the drawers on the bed: the total of my brother's life. The houses, the letter he gave to Rachel, the photographs, these papers. The memories, too. Not many of these, though some appear to be returning. I wonder, briefly, whether any of them are real, or just made up. The photographs, I suppose, prove them real – at least, prove parts of them real.

I begin to sift through the papers. There are bank statements, till slips. There are notebooks with nothing written in them. I go through the bank statements. Some date back twelve years and the newest are from just a few weeks ago. The earliest ones cover the last months of my father's life. There is little in them: payments to supermarkets, pharmacies, petrol stations, electricity bills, water rates. No restaurants, no cinemas. I go through them all. They are stacked in date order. There are some months missing, but not many. A history of my father's and brother's lives in withdrawals and deposits. The money going in is very little. The same amount, more or less, coming out every month.

There are a few items that stand out. About a year after the statements start, there is an entry for a funeral parlour: seven thousand rand. I don't know, I have been out of the country for many years, but it seems like a lot. I picture an ornate coffin, gilded in bronze, flowers overflowing in a church. A priest, his hands held up. In the pews, one man with head bowed. Outside the pall-bearers smoke and mutter to one another, too used to grief to comment on the ornateness of the funeral compared to the scarcity of mourners.

A few months later there is a large sum deposited in Peter's account. It stays there and does not diminish by much. My brother's spending habits do not change. But salary payments into Peter's account stop in 2009 and there is little in the account by the time of the last statement. I see the airfare to London, and I notice something else. Both my father and, after his death, Peter made payments to a company called 24/7 PI. I look them up in the Yellow Pages: a local private investigation firm. I make a note of the address.

I begin going through the till slips. There is little of interest in them. No receipts for funerals or detective agencies. I spend a few minutes looking at one in particular. It is for a can of Coca-Cola — one can. I cannot make out the date, but it seems old. I almost laugh. My brother drank Coke. It doesn't fit. It is too mundane, too carefree, to belong in this house. I keep this receipt, throw the others away.

I open the box. At the top of it is something that takes my breath away. Another photograph, this one more recent than the others I have seen. A photograph of Rachel and me on our wedding day. It is not one of the official photographs. It has clearly been taken from a distance. The background is blurred, though our faces are perfectly in focus. We are looking at each other, smiling, waiting perhaps for the photographer, the official one, to compose his next shot. We are standing on the peace pagoda in Battersea Park. We came here for our photographs after the wedding. We could have had them taken in Richmond, of course, but this was where we had bought our first flat together. This was our place.

We are standing there, my arms around her. She has goose bumps. It is July but it is a cool day. I run my fingers over her arms, remembering the night at the bus stop years before. We are laughing, self-conscious, but in a happy way. We are proud, there is no other word for it, to be with each other, to be watched and envied by strangers. My eye catches a flash of light, sun on a lens perhaps. I look up and notice, though I forget it almost as soon as I see it, until now – a man in the distance, lowering a camera, a tourist, an amateur photographer.

This is the photograph taken a second before the lens was lowered.

I look closely at Rachel. I have never seen her more beautiful. I thought that then too. I touch her face with the tip of my finger. I remember touching her, the touch of her skin. It sends a jolt through me.

The box also contains the receipts for the detective agency. It adds up to a significant amount of money, especially for someone without a salary. There is only one photograph of me and Rachel, but I find my home address, my work address, both my and Rachel's email addresses and a copy of my degree certificate. I pull out an invitation to Rachel's thirtieth birthday party.

It was in our flat. At three in the morning, drunk on our bed after everyone had left. My fingers in her mouth. She had had a cigarette, her last. The taste of it turned me on even more.

When I think of this now, my gaze shifts from the couple on the bed to the corner of the room. Sitting in the chair in the dark, a man, his face invisible. I see him – as if he is real.

The watching. I wonder how long it went on for, how much they knew, how closely I was kept under surveillance. There is a copy of my degree certificate, but were they watching me then or did they get hold of it only recently? Somehow I know the answer. It makes sense. Since leaving, I have never been out of sight, save perhaps for a few months in the beginning. First my father, then Peter, kept watch over me. Why? Did they think they could know me by doing that? Get to the truth of me, the real me?

Perhaps they did. Perhaps they found out what they needed to know. Were they proud of what I achieved? Or perhaps they saw everything presented to them as a lie, some story painted by an amateur detective, and me, the main character, a charlatan, acting for an audience of two. Perhaps they thought that. I will never know.

These cameras in the house, I find myself thinking, somehow meant for me, some sort of lesson or communication.

In a small linen bag I find a watch. On the back a date, then my father's and mother's initials: 2 July 1980. NRH. SGH. Their tenth wedding anniversary. Rachel and I were married on the same date in 2009. It would have been their thirty-ninth anniversary. I have never thought of this until now. Coincidence. I try to remember if I suggested the date or Rachel.

She would have been pleased to know the significance of the date, I know that. It would have made her happy – more happy. Too late.

The watch has the right time on it, though the date has not moved correctly into place. It shows half a six and half a seven. I take off my own and put this on instead. There is a crease in the leather where it has sat in the buckle over the years. I do it up to there and it sits perfectly on my wrist. I wonder if Peter wore it as well as my father.

The contents of the second drawer are mostly rubbish. There are drawing pins, rubber bands, a pair of earphones, the wires frayed. The ordinariness of it. What did he buy drawing pins for? What music did he listen to, if it was music? Perhaps they were bought to listen to meditation tapes. Unlikely. Perhaps his investigator sent a sound recording along with the photograph and the addresses: a recording of the wedding; or, a recording of me asleep, Rachel too.

I think I might find more: my parents' wedding rings, the jewellery my mother used to wear – but there is nothing. There is no safe in the house, it seems. He may have sold the jewellery as he appears to have sold most of the furniture and other belongings. It may have been my father, of course. I imagine him alone in this house. He was always a quiet man, kept to himself, even with his children. But this is too quiet. Too much silence for one man. Five bedrooms, one person. They must have seemed emptier, larger, for the knowledge they used to be filled. Then, him and one other: a grown-up son. Better or worse? The son a constant reminder – another reminder – of what was lost.

Why did he keep the house? The past is baked into the walls. If I stripped away the paint, the coats that I applied and my brother and father must have applied, shadows, scents would be released. The more I strip away, the more the house fills with them, layer upon layer, sifting in the breeze.

At the bottom of the drawer is a brown envelope. There is no writing on the outside. Inside I find more photographs and another envelope, this one sealed. There are three photographs.

The first is of my mother and father. I grow numb when I look at this, when I notice it is them, a wave of coldness, starting at my neck. I do not have any photos of them. No photos of my brothers either. The ones I found here are the first. I have never had any, not since that camera I owned, and not since, after my mother died, my father removed all the photographs from view. This is the first time I have seen my father since I left Port Elizabeth, aged eighteen. My mother before that even. She died in 1987. I was twelve, the age Peter was when Paul died.

They're grinning broadly. It must have been taken before they had children, or at least when we were very young. They are younger than I am now. My mother's hair is being blown to the side. She is wearing large sunglasses. I can still see her eyes – they are laughing. My father has curly hair, though it is already beginning to recede. He is bare-chested. A day at the beach perhaps. I do not recognise the faces. I do, of course, but they are like strangers. At least, these are not the pictures of them I have in my mind, the pictures I can remember. They do not look like this when I picture them.

Around my mother's neck is a string of white beads. Her brown skin. This I remember. I remember rolling the shells – I think that is what they were – around in my fingers. Beneath my fingers her warm skin and the mole at the base of her throat. I look for this but I cannot see it in the photograph. It is not right that I can't see it. I remember it. It should be here. I remember touching it and her pushing me away. Paul was not there. It was after he died. A thought flashes through my mind. This is not my mother. But I know it is, really. The photo is faded. Perhaps the light was at the wrong angle. Perhaps the mole only appeared on her later. I place the photograph on the bedside table.

The more I think about that time, the more I have to admit the memories are fading. They are reflections in a pond. Revisiting them is like dropping a pebble into the water. They break up, disappear. Fallible – the word comes to me.

Maybe it would be for the best if she were not my mother, if they were not my parents. Perhaps they, too, had that thought.

There is something in the photo, these happy, smiling, young faces, that I do not know, that stands over me, looms

– that is the word – over me. Something dark in the looking at it.

The next shows two boys crouched over a dog lying in the road. I close my eyes. We did a lot together, the three of us. When you live in the middle of nowhere, there is no one else to play with, so you stick together. There were just two years between each of us so it was easier. Paul and Peter were closest. The younger of the two wanting to be seen to be older and the eldest, almost a teenager, not wanting to be around children. I was more bookish than them as well – always reading. But we managed well enough. We all loved cricket and played it in the garden together. We rode our bikes. We went exploring, looking for bugs, for snakes in the bush at the back of the house.

They were cruel sometimes, as boys can be. On one of our hunts, as we called them, we went out onto the road. Peter and Paul went up ahead, stood at the fence and looked back at me, running to catch up. They looked only momentarily and then ducked under. The fence running parallel to the road was ornamental and not designed to keep boys in or intruders out.

On the other side, they stopped again to look at me. We were not allowed on the road. We had been told many times. That look was a challenge. I knew that even then. I looked back at the house, but there was no movement in it, no shouts from our mother to come back.

I walked up to the fence, to a part of it a bit further along that was hidden from the house by a tree. I called to them. I cannot remember what I said. I stood there in the shade and watched them on the black strip of tar. Peter had a stick in his hand and they were standing over something in the road. I could not make out what it was and, taking another look back at the house, went to join my brothers.

It was a dog, not a mark on it, at least nothing I could see. Its eyes were closed. I thought – more and more of this scene is coming back to me – it could be asleep. I stepped forward, then knelt by the dog, slowly reaching out a hand. I was dimly aware of my brothers behind me but I was focused on the dog, willing it to open its eyes. Someone, I do not remember whether Peter or Paul, reached out to its haunches and shoved it, making a barking noise at the same time. It was Peter, I remember, and it is him in the picture too. I jumped, but stumbled, falling backwards into Paul's legs. They pushed me forward again and this time I had to put out my hands to stop falling and one of them I placed against the dog's fur. It was still warm, but the flesh beneath was stiffer than it should have been. I remember arms holding me there, touching this animal; me, unsuccessfully, holding my face back from it. I cannot remember what I said, whether I was laughing with them, whether I was screaming at them.

After what was probably just a second or two, they let go and walked off back to the house, Peter's arm around Paul's shoulder, my camera in Paul's hand.

Did I fling stones after them? A detail that could be the product of my adult mind and not a fact that occurred almost thirty years ago. Memories get embellished.

These things were nothing. What boys do. Forgotten five minutes later. Children do not bear grudges.

The third photograph is of Paul. He is sleeping. A photograph taken by a loving parent. His child asleep, growing, replenishing. Any minute now he will open his eyes and smile. He is nine or ten and the time for this is fast running out. Best cherish it. He will reach out, still half asleep, for Mommy or Daddy, and bury his face in their neck.

The boy has golden hair. An angel. I can see this even though the photograph is faded, even though it is almost thirty years old. The hair is parted at the side and falls neatly to the left. He faces straight up from the pillow. He is smiling, as much as you can be in your sleep. I am smiling now too.

Paul, the middle child, was favoured by both Peter and me. He was Peter's closest companion, and he was, in many ways, the boy I wanted to be. Always laughing; almost as tall as Peter. And, when Peter was not around, we played together. It hurt that he would turn to Peter when the three of us were together, but it was natural.

I put the photographs back in the envelope and place that in the drawer. I will keep these. Once everything is done, maybe I will hold on to these.

I hold the other envelope, turn it over. I do not open it, but instead start to walk out of the room. In the doorway I stop, turn around. I go back to the drawer and open it slowly. I take out the photographs again and go back to the last one: Paul. The picture is different now. Where before I could see, could feel in fact, the blood in his veins, feel his breath on my cheek, now it is different. The child is dead; the body in a coffin, or lying on a shelf in a morgue. The camera excludes everything except the boy's face and the cushion beneath it. The picture is taken from the side and above. It excludes the left side of his skull so the viewer cannot see the break. He has been expertly prepared. The hair, too neat for a sleeping child, combed lovingly, for the last time, by my mother – or perhaps by someone else, the morgue attendant, a stranger. It is hard to tell.

How did I miss it? The pallor of the skin, the blueness of the lips. No amount of make-up could ever disguise it.

I wonder about the photographer. I imagine my father. Maybe it was not him, but I picture him nonetheless, his hands shaking slightly, but at the moment he presses the shutter, still. Why would a father do this? How could a father do this? I picture him at the morgue, standing over the body. He wants to reach down to his boy. Take his heart in his hand and squeeze. Maybe, just maybe.

I embellish. The photograph is fading, the boy in it disappearing. I cannot see any of this.

It comes back to me. My father at the pool, Peter in his lap, Paul at his feet. On the rocks above, perched like a vulture, another child, too frightened to cry.

6

I am in the bungalow. I wake up here. At least, I come to consciousness here. I do not remember walking over.

I am in the chair in front of the screen. There is a disc in the laptop and I am watching it. There are hours of footage of me. I paint, sleep, eat.

I get to my feet and walk through the smaller house, going into each room. I press my palms against the walls, knock on them with my fists, listening for an echo.

Later, I return to the cemetery, taking flowers as promised. When I get there, I realise I should have bought more than one bunch. I split the bunch and separate the flowers between the graves, as if doling out sweets to children.

Peter's grave is undisturbed. I do not know what I was expecting but still I find myself thinking this.

The day of Paul's funeral was windy. It is always windy here. A normal day. The wind blew sand into my mouth. It stuck to the wetness on my cheek and dried there. I felt encrusted with dirt.

Opposite me, a woman in black and white – a nun. She was looking at me too. She had her hands clasped together and held out in front of her, praying. I have never been religious, though we went to church every week as a family before Paul died. She smiled at me. I did not smile back. I wanted her gone. Not just away from this place – I wanted her to disappear completely. Who was she to smile at me like that? Doesn't she know what happened? Doesn't she know, this messenger of God?

To my left, Peter, and to his left, our father and mother. I stand apart from Peter, as far away as I could get. He knows what happened, what I saw. Peter, in turn, stands apart from our parents. The gap between me and them a chasm.

There was plastic grass around the grave.

I did not want to stand near them. I was angry with them. With Peter, with my parents too, though I did not know why. What I had seen: Peter, skipping away down the rocks, faster than I could go, me struggling, slipping down the rocks. How could they leave me back there? Why did they run off? I did not know where I was and could see nothing. If they had not left me, things would have been different. Thoughts I had – or have. I cannot tell whether they came to me on the day Paul died, the day of his funeral, or now, standing here, reliving it.

There was a cut on my leg and there was pus and it was leaking into my sock. Standing at the grave, I could feel it hardening.

I still have a scar on my knee from that day at the river. Another on my chin.

I force myself to try to remember the details. Of the death,

I mean. It is of the utmost importance. It is of the utmost importance, it seems to me, to remember everything, every detail. If I can, then this feeling that has been with me since I got Paul's letter in London might go away. The feeling that something is not right.

I have not thought about it. I've tried not to think about it for so long it is difficult now. I will probably not be able to remember all the details, all the facts. The older I get, the further away from the truth I recede. Perhaps. Things are changing, shifting. I remember details but I ask myself if they are made up, or some of them at least, and the question doesn't go away. I want to and, if I am honest with myself, have wanted to for some time, bang my head against a wall, over and over again, until it all comes back, until it comes back or goes away, forever.

I go through it – methodically is the word that comes to mind.

The setting is a series of pools in a mountain river near Barrydale, a town in the Karoo.

It is as if it is different people.

These people arrived and drove to the cottage they were renting. It was hot and there was no swimming pool and they had heard about the rock pools up in the pass.

After parking their car – a Chevrolet – at a viewpoint, they picked their way through gorse on the slope of the mountain, moving slowly into the valley. There were five of them. The man, who carried a basket, was in front, followed by two children, his wife with the third child in the rear.

The father held the basket in front of him. The child behind him, Peter, had to catch the branches as they flew back. It seemed to be a sort of game. Peter was becoming a man. He had to show this.

Behind him, Paul. It is harder to see him. The picture is faded.

The youngest child lagged behind and the mother called to him, or shouted.

Their path led out from the bush onto rocks by the side of the river. The youngest was the last to emerge and he walked between the members of his family, looking up at them, their attention elsewhere.

The party laid out their picnic at the uppermost pool. It was the largest and the warmest, they thought, and there was space on the rocks to sit. The mother had a camera with her. It belonged to one of the boys – the youngest, me. But she was using it. He did not mind. He said he did not mind. It was new. It was a deal they had. It was his camera – a birthday present – but she would use it sometimes and she would show him how to use it properly too and maybe one day he would be a photographer and she would buy all the film he wanted, of course. He liked their arrangement, but maybe she was using it a little bit too much now. She was taking pictures. The father told her she was wasting film. It was easy to tell he was not being serious, was just humouring her.

She took photos of the boys mainly. Of the three of them together, or in pairs, when they weren't looking. In one, the two older boys were standing with their arms around each other's shoulders, posing for the camera. The eldest was flexing his left bicep, his face in a grimace. In the background of that photograph, the third boy slipped into shot. Facing the camera, features blurred. He is not meant to be there.

After a while, the two boys went off, followed by the youngest. 'Look after your brother,' the mother called. Or did she? Do I remember those words or do I think of them just because they are the obvious ones to say?

The two older boys set off down the path. The youngest followed. The path led through thick bush – thick, at least, to a child.

He kept up with them for a while, but the path was steep and uneven underfoot and he had to push his way through branches that scratched at his face.

He began to lose them. He lost sight of them, could not hear them either. He stopped and looked around him. The sun, the bush, the cicadas.

He began to move again and he called out too, but as he did he stumbled and fell to the ground. That must be where the cuts came from, though I cannot see them.

There was a noise from down the path and the eldest came back and looked at him and said something. Or, he said nothing and just looked. The youngest was quiet too, his voice stopped by the expression on his brother's face. He was left alone. He turned and looked back. He could not see his parents. He heard a voice, he thought, or was it a bird? Nothing else. He looked back down the path, down the trail of white rocks disappearing around a corner and into the deep blue of the sky.

He wanted to go back to his parents. He wanted to be sitting on the rocks with his mother and father, sitting between them. He didn't want to be here, but he had been told to go and now he couldn't go back on his own.

What did he do next, as he got to his feet, what did he see? I try to remember, try to put myself back in the skin of the boy, try to imagine myself there. It is hard. Twenty-eight years. I close my eyes and try to think myself there. But it has gone.

There was a policeman at the funeral as well as a nun: the law for this world and the next. No, not a man – a policewoman – standing back in the crowd. I could not see her, of course. But I knew she was there. Know she was there. A courtesy. And then afterwards, at the wake, I went out of the house. I did not want to be there any more. Did not want to be surrounded by these people, who all seemed to want to kiss me, or pat my head like I was a dog. I went out and down to the bottom of the garden where I could not be seen. The rain had stopped. I sat on a rock behind another rock. The irony is not lost on me. I sat there and then I saw the policewoman. She was smoking. I watched her for a long time before I was seen in turn. She seemed to get a shock as if she had seen a ghost. But then she nodded and said hello.

She came over and stood a few metres away. I try to remember what she said, how the conversation went. I do not remember her talking, do not remember answering. I wanted to tell her everything. But I said nothing. I stared at her, just stared and eventually she gave up trying to talk to me.

She held out her hand instead. A good person.

We walked back to the house. I held her hand. It was a long way for me. I did not want to go inside. I wanted to tell her something, this person who held my hand and did not push me to say something. I wanted to tell her something, everything. I had seen everything after all. But everything was too much to tell. Would it have made a difference if I had spoken? Would that have rescued things somehow or harmed them even more?

But I could not talk. The words would not form themselves.

She delivered me inside and I watched as she got into her car and drove off. I watched her go and drive up the road and I waited at the window for a long time for her to come back. But she never did.

I wonder where she is now. She will be in her late fifties or early sixties. Perhaps I have passed her in the street without realising. Perhaps, as we passed, she sensed something, turned and looked after me as I carried on, unknowing.

'Paul Hyde. Beloved son and brother. 15 June 1973 to 11 December 1983.' I read it again and again.

Apart from when I was here for Peter's funeral, I have never been back to Paul's grave. My parents, and later my father on his own, must have visited the grave, but I was never taken. At least, I cannot remember being taken.

I wonder if Peter ever came here. If he did, what would he have felt? Guilt can be a strange thing. It can give birth to ghosts. Out of the grey dust, bones begin to form, then the flesh on the bones. The wind blows it away almost as fast as it forms, but in the end he comes to see, in the half light, his brother in the dust. He comes to see all that has been taken.

What would things have been like if we had not lost touch, Peter and I? What if I had come home, maybe a few years after I left? Patched things up, maybe together we'd have agreed on a different story. I could have flown in, driven from the airport to Peter's house. In the morning we would have come here together. Afterwards a coffee, a drink in a bar, a walk on a beach. We would have left our families behind for this.

A fairytale.

I have never been back.

I remember now. It comes to me. Dad used to come here all the time after Mom died. He asked me once to come with him and I said no. I shook my head, in fact. I did not say anything. He went on his own. He would have stood here, where I stand now. Would he wonder why his two remaining sons did not want to go with him? They each had their own reasons. Perhaps the reasons were a mystery to him. Perhaps he held back, fearing if he spoke out he would uncover an unspeakable horror at the heart of it.

I left South Africa in 1993. I was eighteen. The idea was a gap year, though I knew it would be longer than that. I had a British passport. It would be easy to stay away.

I left in the morning to catch a flight to Johannesburg, from where I would fly to London. My father drove me to the airport and left me at the passenger drop-off point. He did not park and come into the terminal building with me. I said nothing, of course, and did not complain when he told me the plan. I just shrugged. He said it was practical, that the airport would be too busy. We both knew that was not true. This was Port Elizabeth after all. My father got out of the car and unloaded my backpack from the boot. He stood before me. I sensed he wanted to hug me, or, at least, was thinking that he should. This was hard for him. Hard for me too. I could have made it easier. I held out my hand. My father hesitated, only for half a second, then held his out. 'Good luck.' I don't remember the words. It could have been anything. It was brief, though. I stood on the pavement and watched while my father got in the car and drove off. Part of me wanted to run after him. Or, at least, lift up my arm so he could see in the rearview mirror that I was waving and perhaps he would have smiled. I am sure he didn't smile.

I did not say goodbye to Peter either. He also left home at eighteen, four years before me. After two years in the army, he had returned to Port Elizabeth and was working as a waiter. He lived in a flat with three others. I had not seen the flat, just heard the odd word from my father. There was some talk of a course at the technikon. But nothing came of it. I didn't take any interest in what he did. We hadn't seen each other for around six months by then. My father tried to persuade me to go round there the week before I left. I did not answer and it was not mentioned again.

I go back to the airport – try to. I try to go back to the handshake and look into my father's eyes. I have never really thought of him as a man with internal contradictions and emotions. They never reached the surface at least. Or perhaps I just do not remember. I know now, if I did not know then, that he knew I wouldn't be coming back. Of course he did. He was not stupid. Why would I come back? Two men in a house, one other in the same city, all that is left of a family in which a son and brother had been killed and a wife and mother died when her car went off a cliff. And the blame – for there was blame, there is blame – shifts from man to man to man. Why wouldn't the two remaining sons want to get as far away as possible? He was lucky, if you can call it that, they stayed until they were eighteen.

I put myself in the car with my father on the drive back to the house. In his thoughts. Ten years is all it took. First a son, then a wife. Then two more sons. Not dead but, let's face it, they might as well be. They had made their choices. He had tried to get through to them ever since the day Paul died in the accident. Peter and Paul were always daring each other to do things. It was an accident. What else would it be? He had tried. And what was waiting for him at the end of the road? An empty house, devoid of everything that had once filled his life. I imagine the car coasting to a stop and my father leaning forward over the steering wheel – and then nothing. I lose sight of him at this point.

I wrote, of course. My father wrote me a letter about a month after I arrived in London, giving me news of events in the city, the cricket match he'd attended, what he was growing in the garden. Those sorts of things, I seem to remember. I replied. There were other letters every month or so.

After two years, I had managed to enrol at university and I stopped writing back. I didn't tell him about the university. I thought he might ask me why I didn't come back, thinking he might say universities in South Africa were every bit as good as those in the UK. But that's not why I stopped, not really. I was making my own way, getting further away from them and they no longer had a right to know.

He carried on writing for a while after I stopped, but then he stopped too. I checked my PO Box every now and then, but nothing. Nothing by email either, though my father probably did not use email. It was still very new. Of course I could be mistaken about that. Why would I have known, after all?

Soon after I graduated, I checked again and there was a letter, but not from him. It was from a lawyer, stating that my father had died: a heart attack. The letter was postmarked four weeks earlier. I had missed the funeral. Not that I would have gone, but now I had no choice.

It was winter and there I was, standing in a post office in Earls Court, around me crowds of people. But it was silent where I was. The world was still. I looked for another letter. I thought maybe there'd be one from Peter. For a time I found myself actually wanting one. I came back every day for a month. But I did not really expect one and did not receive one. I did get another letter from the lawyer, saying the estate had been left to Peter. I did not reply, did not try to get in touch at all. There was nothing to be said.

I was in a pub in Camden the night after I got the letter announcing his death. Someone pushed me. Or I pushed him,

I forget. I am not exactly a regular fighter, but I have a size advantage over most. I swatted his arm away as he pushed me and then punched him on the nose with my right fist. At first he had just been an annoyance, but something took over then. I lost myself, felt my fist go into his face, the cartilage scrape against bone. Felt the blood, the warmth, the stickiness of it, though that was later. The man went down. The crowd parted. I went after him. It was not enough. I went for him and took him by the shirt and punched him in the face again – and again. Like punching a pool of mud. A fourth time. He escaped my grasp somehow and crawled away. I stood there, a piece of his shirt in my hand, my own shirt spattered with blood. The pub was quiet. I was on my own, didn't know anyone there. Just drinking. No one stopped me leaving, no one came after me. I walked south, sat on a park bench near Euston station and held my fist – I think it was still clenched – in my other hand and sat there until dawn.

I had tried for years to forget my family: the silences, the things unspoken wedged between us, Peter's part in Paul's death that he never seemed to acknowledge and was never brought into the open – for which he had me to thank. I thought I had succeeded. But my father's death altered that, broke the scum on the surface of the pond. Just one left now. I remember wishing they had both died at the same time. I would be free of them then, and the hold they had on me.

It was a setback but no more. Seven years after my father's death, I met Rachel. By then I was sure it was all over. I had forgotten these people, my family. I had friends. Not many admittedly, as the bank took up most of my time. But now I had Rachel. Rachel took it all away. I left it all behind, properly this time. Leaving Port Elizabeth had been just the first step. I sloughed off the skin of my past. Not just the skin, the bones, blood and gristle of it too. A lizard, shedding everything until just spirit, emerging anew from the undergrowth.

I have brought the letter with me. I had put it back in the drawer, but as I sat in the car, my hands on the steering wheel, I decided to go back for it. I place my hand into the pocket of my trousers and feel it there. I will read it, but now doesn't seem like the right time. I know it is for me, or relates to me. There is nothing on the envelope to say it is for me, but I sense it. Everything in this house is for me, everything relates to me, everything means something to me. I can feel it – the creep of my family, the rising stench of them, the corpses floating, drifting upwards through years of silt to rest, rotten, on the surface.

That first letter from Peter I received in London in March 2011. Once read it could not be forgotten. I had to come back, though I did not know it then, did not know it for a while. That was the first bubble in the pond, the first sign something was coming. I remember the day. Snow. Rachel. A snowball down her shirt. And then later, undressing her, the wetness on her back, the soft hairs. I kissed her, and then I remembered the letter. At least, it shifted from the back to the front of my mind. She asked if something was wrong. The coldness in my stomach. Perhaps I should have told her then. Why didn't I?

I cannot think why I didn't. It was the logical thing to do, the sort of thing a husband would tell his wife.

I left them, but perhaps they never really left me – always watching over my shoulder. There, watching me graduate from King's, standing silent in the back row as I married Rachel, and in the corner of the darkened room when the letter dropped onto the mat. I should have been able to smell them.

A letter from my brother, the man in many ways responsible for all this, taunting me. I couldn't just leave it, couldn't just forget it.

And then the second letter, and nothing in that to atone for his part in this either, somehow managing, I don't know how he did it, to imply that he was the wronged one, me the despicable liar. And then saying, implying again, what he was going to do, and leaving me no choice but to follow him so as to put things right, so as to save him, to save him once again.

I am angry with myself for not bringing more flowers.

I am not Jewish, but I take twelve stones, three for each member of my family, and place them on the gravestones.

Goodbye.

I do not look back.

7

I walk through the rooms of the red-brick house. The smell of paint is fading and underneath it the old smell is coming back. Faint, but now that I notice it, it seems to get stronger and stronger. I feel ill. The smell baked into all the layers of paint and soaked deep into the plaster, deep into the brick.

In the bedroom I stand in front of the bed. There is a hollow on one side of it; on the other a smaller hollow. Again I wonder about a family. There is no evidence of one. No pictures on the walls, no photographs other than the old ones I have found. Perhaps that was it, though, a divorce, uncontested. All the furniture went with the wife and children to their new house in Cape Town or Johannesburg. Perhaps in one of the drawers I have not been through I will find a number or an old mobile phone.

I do not think it likely, though. A sister-in-law, nieces, nephews – this place does not seem like it contains the memories of a different offshoot of the family. It is empty of that.

Perhaps the hollow is from my mother. Perhaps the bed has not been changed. Perhaps in here I could find flakes of my parents' skin, and put them together piece by piece. A human jigsaw.

I find little things that I should do to the house: patches I have missed, paint splashes to clean off windows, cracks to fill in. But I leave it all, at least for now. My heart is not in it. It has beaten me. That is the thought that comes to me. Eroded what I had left, what I had built up, like acid.

I stand in front of the kitchen window drinking a glass of water. I drink it without stopping. I cannot remember the last time I drank. I pour another and drink this one more slowly.

I lie in bed with the curtains open. The moonlight picks out my shape under the sheets. I lie still, listening to the crickets and the night birds. It's like I have never left. These sounds are part of me. They are what I went to sleep with when I was learning about the world. They're at once comforting and unsettling, a reminder of the time before. But also they sound out of time, as if I have shifted through time and, as I lie here, so too do the children lie in their rooms with our mother and father sitting downstairs watching TV, reading the papers. I can hear the television. What will they do if they come up here and find a strange man in their bed? Will they recognise me as their son, the same child, as they once said, who just could not stop telling stories? Or would they take a stick to me, set on me with kitchen knives?

I put my hand to my face and there I can feel the scar, the one on my chin. I return to that day in the mountains.

I slipped on the path and cried out and Peter came back. Just for a second. He came back and saw what had happened and then he turned around and ran again and by then Paul was standing on the ledge, looking down at the water. Too far to jump.

He had beaten Peter to the ledge, because Peter had come back for me. Peter was older. He should have been first.

My fists were clenched at my sides. I was further up the path now and could see them through the bush, just a glimpse of them if I crouched slightly.

Peter's hand on Paul's back. Around his shoulder. Or, his hand in the centre of his back, muscles tensed.

Their brown backs in the sun. Bones sticking through the skin.

I rubbed the grit off my legs and arms. No cuts yet. No blood. Just scrapes.

I surprise myself with what I remember, what I don't remember. I remember things like this, things like Peter's hand on Paul's back. Most of all I want to see the seconds after this. I want to see it again – what happened. But I cannot.

I weigh each word. I attempt to place the figures exactly where they were. Precisely here on this rock, a hand held precisely there, the little finger on a shoulder blade, the palm centred on a mole. Each time I do, the figure shifts, the hand moves, just a little, moves while my gaze is averted. The words, the pictures they form, play tricks on me. I pin them down again, but it is no use. People of water.

I sit in the chair to read the letter. The envelope is sealed. I break it open and inside is another envelope with my name on it, nothing else. John Hyde, the formality of the surname. I am not sure which I notice first, that it is addressed to me or that, after all this time, I am able to recognise my father's handwriting. The last time I saw it, I was perhaps twenty. I turn it over a few times before opening it.

5 October 1999

Dear John

Many times I have been on the verge of getting in touch. I have known about you for some time, about your life. I have spent money on a private detective. I hope you do not regard this as an invasion of your privacy.

The detective told me about your travels. You must have seen a lot and have many stories to tell. He told me too how you were accepted into King's College and how well you are doing. Graduating at the top of your class at such an institution is a wonderful achievement. I had not heard of it but I asked the detective and he said it had a good reputation and then I went to the library and did some research. I am proud of you. Your mother would have been as well.

I was not surprised to hear you were studying literature. You were always a reader and blessed with an imagination none of the rest of your family seemed to share. Not much money in it but I am sure you will find your way. You have an iron will in you. I have always known it, always seen it. It is commendable, in many ways, and will take you far.

In the end I did not get in touch. I respect your decision to stay away. I understand it too, as much as I can. Your sensitivity – this is how I explain it. You were always more sensitive than the rest of us. The loss of Paul and your mother: it is understandable that you had to get away and make a fresh start, cut off reminders of the past. As much as I wanted to see you, I could not call you back. I had to wait for you, wait for you to decide to return. In the end, I could not wait long enough.

I am sorry we lost contact. But I do not blame you for this. I want you to know that I do not blame you for anything, no matter what I might write in this letter, no matter what you might have thought in the past. I never have. There was no blame to be attributed after all. No blame in an accident.

I am writing with a request. I do not wish to sound melodramatic but I have only a few months left. If I make the next century it will be only to experience the first short weeks of it. The doctors say I will become less lucid, less able to do things like write letters or have coherent thoughts.

I have an inoperable tumour in my brain. I have known for some time now. I do not fear what comes. It comes to us all. I am not so old to have already made my peace with death, but I am old enough for it not to be a surprise. Sixty. Not exactly a match-winning innings but a reasonable score. I am being treated well, and I am not alone. I have your brother.

Peter and I are talking again. Though we are not as close as some fathers and sons, we have become closer recently. He has been good to me. After you left, it took a while but he came round for lunch one day and since then we have been on stable ground. And once I told him about the cancer he started coming round more often, every few days in fact. He has even asked to move back in with me. I will consider it as no doubt it will be a help and a comfort to have him here.

It will be a help to him as well. He is working as a chef in a hotel on the coast. It is not very well paid and living without the burden of rent will make his pay cheque go further.

I have decided to leave the house and what's left of the estate after my medical bills have been paid to Peter. There will not be a great deal. Perhaps just enough for a small investment property. I hope you are not upset by this. It is partly because I hear you are doing so well and have no concerns for your future. The money, especially after being converted into pounds, would mean little to you. Peter, on the other hand, has not applied himself to anything. This is his second job in two years and I am concerned he will not make a go of it. He is not wasteful of money, does not do drugs, at least as far as I know. He just does not appear to be interested. As if there is always something else on his mind other than what he is doing.

There is still time of course – he is only twenty-eight. I live in hope.

I will ask him to send this letter to you. It will be sealed of course. Perhaps he would not agree if he knew exactly what was in it. I hope he will not let me down. I could have my lawyer send it but the purpose of it would not be served that way. I hope – perhaps against hope – that the letter will lead to a reconciliation between the two of you.

I will ask him to wait until after my death, and until after the estate has been settled before sending it. I do not want my death or distractions over the will to get in the way of what I am trying to say, what I am trying to achieve. It is for that reason I will ask that you be told my death was due to a heart attack and happened very quickly, so your judgement and your next actions will not be falsely motivated.

So here it is (a simple thing to ask, less simple to carry out): I hope that you can find it within yourself to write to him. Perhaps even to come and see him.

I have asked the same of him, without mentioning that I was writing to you. He has said he will think about it. It is hard to tell if he means it.

I want you two to get back on speaking terms and for you to forgive each other. The two of you are all that's left. Family was very important to your mother. To me too, of course. But if you won't do this for me, perhaps you will do it for her.

I use the word forgive and do not use it lightly. You two were never the same after Paul's death. Your mother and I tried to bring you back but it seemed like there was something between the two of you. You were silent when together. Two foxes circling each other, tails bristling. Or, better, two north magnetic poles: we pushed you together, but as soon as we let you go you pushed each other away.

Forgive what, you may ask. It is hard for me to answer this. I have been trying to answer it ever since Paul died. I am not sure I have the answer even now. In an accident there is nothing to forgive.

The change in Peter after Paul's death was profound. Before, he was the happiest boy you could wish to know. You were more thoughtful, sometimes a bit sulky even, but you were young, more introspective. Your brothers were quite boisterous with you, though they loved you of course. There were some moments when your mother and I would have our hearts broken by seeing the three of you, your arms around each other. I remember one day you fell off your bike. There was a rope in the middle of the road. I think you were playing cops and robbers. You went over it, your bike flipped, you went flying. Peter and Paul rushed up to you – I saw it happen from the other end of the garden – and they gave you a big hug and tried to stop you crying. I carried you inside and they came too and sat beside you holding your hand as your Mom wiped away the blood. That was one of those moments.

Perhaps they did the same on the day Paul died. You

had quite a cut on your leg. On your chin too. Perhaps
you called for Paul. You used to do that. You would call
for him to help you. You adored him, looked up to him –
to Peter too – in spite of the rough-housing. There were
times Peter (more than Paul) found it annoying, but that
is to be expected. He was twelve, you were eight, that is
all the reason needed.

You would have cried out, I'm sure. You never told us
how you got those cuts and scrapes, though I suppose
it was not the first thing on anyone's mind. There was
blood all over the place and most of it was Paul's. That
you were cut seemed of little concern.

Once again I digress.

It made your mother and I ache to think what you
had gone through. Both of you. Peter especially. Jumping
at the same time. I imagine – he would never admit it –
he felt guilty. As if he was responsible. But he was not. It
was an accident.

Even if one pushed the other, it was an accident.
There was no pushing anyway, was there? You were too
far away to see. You said you were further up the path
when they went over.

Sometimes it was hard remembering it was an
accident. It was like you two had a secret from that day
on. Something you would not talk to us about. I wonder,
did you talk to each other about it? I think not. What
was it, John, this secret? Or did we imagine it? It is
possible we did, probable even.

We were never the same, either, your mother and I. The death of a child makes you see the world in a different way. Perhaps it caused us to see you differently too. I am sorry for that.

We failed you. And Peter. No matter what really happened that day, we failed you. We tried to talk to you after the accident, to talk about what you had seen, might have seen. One of those times, perhaps it was the last time I tried, to my regret, you said something. You were turned away from me, sat on the edge of your bed, turned away from me, and you said something and I asked you to repeat it and you did and the words were 'I said, I saw.' I saw. Those simple words. They stunned me. They silenced me completely. Silenced both of us. We sat there, not touching and these words were between us and I had to leave. I understood them, of course, understood the bare words, but what they meant, what they might mean, I could not grasp. Would not, perhaps.

To my regret, I say again. I had to leave because there was this thing in the room I knew was there but could not see, could not name, could not bear to look at. I know you wanted to carry on talking, but I could not be there. What did you mean, John? What did you see? Did you see Peter push Paul? Is that what you meant?

I ask, but I ask knowing I will not get a reply, do not deserve a reply, and that is why I can ask.

I had an idea what you meant, of course. We both did, your mother and I. But we could never speak it, speak of it, though it was with us all the time in this house, immovable.

I am reminded of a paradox. An irresistible force meets an immovable object.

I still cannot talk about it. Peter and I never speak of Paul. I don't want to know. I don't think I ever wanted to know. Boys will be boys. You push. You're rough. And then you two never spoke. Your silence made us think there was more to the story. Our little boy who loved to make up stories suddenly went quiet. You did not talk to us, did not talk to your brother, did not talk to him ever again beyond a few perfunctory phrases. Your silence needed to be filled. How could we not fill it? We failed you with our own silence. Better to know. Always better to know.

Your mother's death hit Peter hard too. I think he suspected the truth. You were too young, I think – twelve. He worked it out, though. A car crash, the car off the road on Sir Lowry's Pass, where she had no reason to be. No skid marks. The middle of the day. He found out she was not wearing a seatbelt. I'm not sure how, I tried to shield him from it all. Though it was not law like it is today, your mother always wore her seatbelt. She was dead and there was no letter, so there was no proof it was suicide but the signs were clear.

There could only have been one reason for your mother doing what she did. The death of a child – there's no coming back from that. I am sure Peter already felt guilty about Paul's death and this made it worse.

I am sorry if this is news to you. Perhaps I should have left this in silence too. I do not know what you know. The moment that marks out your children passing over into adulthood: when you know you do not know everything about them. With you it happened too early, far too early.

You were her favourite. It is not something a parent should admit to – having favourites. She did, though she kept it hidden from the others. Your quietness, your love of stories. She studied English Literature too, as you know. (Was that why you chose that course?) And then after, she tried so hard to get back to that place, to get back to you, to the boy, the angel she loved. She tried so hard, John. You may not even remember. Every night she took you to bed and lay there with you and read you stories. She would ask you what you thought of them, what you would do if you were one of the characters. Your answers were brief, uninterested even, though I think there were more ideas in your head than you let on. Every night, until the end.

It was quite recently that Peter asked about you. It was as if he was reading my mind. I had told him the week before about the cancer. I had been thinking about you, thinking about writing this letter, and one afternoon he came right out and asked. 'How is John?' It was as if he knew I had been keeping tabs on you. I answered, 'He seems to be doing OK.' Your brother looked at me for a second and then nodded. I didn't really know what it meant, that nod. Could have been anything.

I told him everything. I told him everything you had been doing, where you lived, which course you were studying. He did not comment on why I was keeping track of you. Sensitive in his own way, too.

He thinks of you often. Though it was only that once he mentioned you, I can tell he thinks of you. When we sit in silence after a meal, I look at him. Sometimes he catches me looking, sometimes not. It seems to make him uncomfortable, so I try not to. I see him and I can tell what he is thinking about. You. You appear, as if real, as if a ghost. It doesn't help that you two look so much alike. You hang there between us. Not Paul, not your mother. You. He looks to you. You stand in judgement over him, it seems. You. His whole life – and perhaps this is why he has achieved so little – lived in this shadow, this shadow of whatever it was you may or may not have seen all those years ago.

It may be too late but my hope is – I return to my request – that you find it in yourself to soften towards him, to remove judgement, if that is what it is, to save what is left of our family. Paul is gone. I have no idea what happened that day, whether Peter pushed him (I hate writing those words) or not, but perhaps it does not matter any more, perhaps it is best forgotten. Perhaps, after all, nothing happened. The silence was just silence. Stunned after your brother's death. Two boys, daring each other, jumped. One hit his head on rocks and broke his neck. The other almost drowned. Nothing.

I still see him, you know – Paul. It is not something

one would admit in polite society. I see him here in the house. I see him running through the sprinkler, hear his laughter, see him curled up at the other end of the couch. I see him asleep, this golden boy, feel the warm breath from his mouth as I lean in to kiss him.

I live with ghosts here, but I have never wanted them gone. That is why I have kept the house all these years, even though it is too big for me (you may be wondering). These visions. This house contains everything I love, everything I have loved. I could not have got rid of it.

The day you left was not my proudest moment. I should have come in to the terminal with you instead of leaving you outside. I did, in fact. I turned the car around and parked and went inside, but you had gone through security and I asked them to let me through. I caused a bit of a scene actually, but they refused and it was all I could do to persuade them to allow me to stay and watch your plane take off.

I am not sure what I would have achieved, but it would have been better to say a proper goodbye.

I wish you well. I hope you continue to be a success and I hope one day you, too, will marry and have children. Maybe you will even mention their grandfather to them, in a kindly way. I would have loved grandchildren. But it was not to be. I have had much joy in my life and many happy years. The years before Paul died with the five of us in this big house were more than most people get, more than most deserve. I loved what we had, all of us, out here in this windswept corner of nothing, our own familial Eden.

I hope one day you, too, will know such a time.

Love Dad

The fifth of October 1999. Twelve years ago. I was twenty-four, recently graduated, and had just been taken on at Lloyds. I had not had any contact with my father or brother for at least four years. I go through the numbers. My father died twelve years ago. I last saw him and Peter eighteen years ago. It sounds too long. Eighteen years – a lifetime. I think back over what I have done in that time. What I haven't done. I made a lot of money. I met Rachel. It is not much.

And during that time, during those eighteen years, my father and my brother, here, sitting where I am, watching over me from afar. My father with that doubt he should never have had. He should have had the truth, no matter how hard.

I sit in the chair with the letter in my hand. After a while it slips and falls to the floor.

For a long time I stare out of the window at a spot at the edge of the garden. I stare, while around me the heat haze breaks up the garden, the house, the sky. They swirl above me, forming, reforming. Everything I can see floats, drifts away.

I can see this, I can describe it because I see it as if from afar, as if I am perched halfway up the wall, looking down on a man sitting crumpled in a chair, a man who does not look like me at all, a man half my size, crushed by the walls that surround him.

8

I sit sweating in the chair in the bungalow. For a second I am adrift. I do not know where I am, and how I got here. I focus on the screen. A man reads a letter. The screen begins to jump, as if the man is trembling.

I feel in my pockets but there is nothing in them. I run next door and into the lounge. The letter lies on the floor next to the chair. I pick it up again and read it. The same words appear. I fold it carefully and place it back in the envelope.

I get into the shower and am standing under the water, my eyes closed, when I hear a crash from the ground floor. I jump out and run down the stairs and into the kitchen. I am naked and still dripping from the shower. There on the floor, below the sink and an open window, a broken glass lies shattered. The curtain flaps in the breeze. My breathing slows.

I move my foot and step on a piece of glass. Wincing, I hold the foot up and watch as a drop of blood falls to the floor. As it lands, I notice, out of the corner of my eye, a footprint, wet, the size of a child's.

I raise my eyes and there is another. The first is fading already. I look further and there is a third and a fourth, and I cannot tell whether I am watching them being formed or whether in fact I am seeing them, one after the other, so that it only seems as if there is an invisible child making them.

I follow the footprints out the door. They are fading. At the door to the outside, I look behind me. Perhaps the child has sneaked behind and is standing right here, over my shoulder. I feel around with my arms like a blind man. But nothing.

When I turn back, I see the footprints cross the concrete floor of the yard and enter the shed.

I listen but there is no sound.

It takes a few moments for my eyes to adjust to the dark. There are tools, a bench, tins. On the table is an old fish tank, its sides split. I step into the shed and peer into the tank. At the bottom, half buried in sand, there is something, I don't know what – a leaf, a dead insect. I put my finger to it, shift it out of the sand. A frog – dead, dried out.

There is nothing here. Four walls. No cupboards. No space to hide.

I am standing in the shed with Peter. It is his fish tank. I am ten. Peter, fourteen, is too old to be collecting frogs. He is looking into the tank and he removes the corpse of one of them. He holds it up. It is as dry as a leaf and has been dead for days, if not weeks. I can tell that even at ten. Yet he is crying. I can see his face now. There are tears in his eyes. I am surprised. Over this?

I want to talk to him, want to say something to him.

Something more than about a frog. Something that matters. I start. I open my mouth but nothing comes out. As I open it, he turns away. He turns away from me and faces the wall, fists at his sides. He whispers. I lean in to hear. He says one word over and over. I cannot make it out. 'Murderer.' It might be that. Again and again. Said so many times it loses its meaning, if it was even that word in the first place.

I try to remember if I had promised to look after his frogs, perhaps to catch flies for them. I do not think so.

But I knew he was talking about himself – if it was that word he used. I might as well not have been there at all.

I walk out of the shed, backwards, so I can keep an eye on him. He does not move. Just the sound. It grows louder as I move closer to the door.

And as I copy those movements twenty-six years later, I am blinded by the sunshine outside the shed. I panic – that's the only word for it. Just for a second. I am gripped by a sudden fear of losing my sight. Of having my eyes plucked out like Gloucester. Stuck here, unable to see, unable to reach a phone. And behind me a person, a person who doesn't want me here, watching me, watching me gasp for water, then shrivel up. Waiting for me to die. The first thing to go is my lips, the water sucked out of them so they draw back from my gums, my yellow teeth exposed to the sun and the dust.

I go through every room on the upstairs floor and close the windows. I do the same downstairs and make sure all the doors are locked. I go out through the garage door and lock that behind me, too. I have not been concerned about security, but now I find myself closing a window, locking it, then coming back two minutes later to make sure it is shut. At the back of my mind I know I will need more than locks. It pains me when a thought, unbidden, flashes through my mind: it is Peter I need to keep out.

I wait in the car outside the address I have for the funeral parlour. Not the one I used, but the one who issued the receipt I found in the drawer. Number 144. It is boarded up. Above the windows a sign has been painted over in grey. Beneath the paint I can make out the words, 'Kemp and Sons Funeral Directors'. There is a phone box nearby. I dial the number I have, but get only an out of order signal. I listen to it for a long time.

I drive into the city and park on Kirkwood Street. The buzzer on the door to number 33 doesn't work. I push the door and it opens. A security guard is behind a desk at the end of a corridor.

'24/7 Detective agency?'

The man points to the board behind him. The agency is on the 5th floor.

'Sign please.'

I sign and head towards the lifts.

'Out of order.' The guard points towards the stairs.

By the time I reach the top, I am out of breath. I am letting myself go.

The inside of the office is in better condition than the building. There is a carpet, a couch, a television, magazines.

It reminds me of a doctor's waiting room. The receptionist is young. She smiles at me.

'Good afternoon. Welcome. Do you have an appointment?'

'I don't. I want to talk to someone about a case.'

'There is no one here at the moment. The detective will be back in about half an hour.'

'I will wait.'

She nods. 'Please.' She points to the couch.

I watch the TV. It is the first time I have seen a television programme in weeks. It is a soap opera, a local one. The volume is turned down.

About forty minutes later, the door opens and a man walks in. He looks down at me and gives half a nod. I think I see him hesitate. Perhaps he recognises me, or at least recognises my brother in me.

He is about fifty, has close-cropped hair and a large chest. He looks like an ex-policeman. I try to think back to the day of the wedding, the tourist taking a photograph and I can see the flash of light on the camera but no further than that. I can't see the figure holding the camera. I don't suppose it was this man, though it is not impossible he would have flown over to London to keep watch on me.

The man talks to the receptionist, then goes into his office. The woman looks back at her computer screen.

I get up from the couch and stand in front of her. She looks up, smiles.

'Can I see him now?'

'I will check.'

She picks up the phone, holds it to her ear, says nothing. Then she returns the receiver. 'Mr De Villiers will see you.'

I go into the office. The man behind the desk rises and holds out his hand without saying a word. We shake and the detective gestures towards a seat.

'How may I help?'

I say nothing for a few seconds. I have not planned this moment.

'I want to find out about a case you are working on.'

'Which case is that?'

'You were engaged by Peter Hyde.'

'Ah.'

'And my father before him.'

He nods, holds the palms of his hands up. 'I was working for Mr Hyde. I am not any more.'

'When did you stop working for him?'

'Several months ago. He said he was going to England. But you understand I am not able to discuss cases with you. We are not doctors, but we have standards too.'

'The case was about me. To follow me.'

'I know.'

I pause for a minute, shake my head. 'I don't want to know about the case as such. I don't care about it. I want to know about him.'

'Your brother?'

'Yes, I want to know. I want to know what he was like.'

'Was?' He raises an eyebrow.

'He is dead.'

The detective pauses. He does not seem shocked. 'I am sorry to hear that.'

'You can help?'

The man looks blankly at me.

I begin to feel I have wasted my time coming here. What will this man be able to tell me after all?

'Did he tell you why he wanted to find me?'

'I didn't enquire about his reasons. I just followed instructions.'

'What was he like?'

'What do you mean, what was he like? He was your brother.'

I want to say, 'Was he happy? Did he smile? Did he have friends, was he involved with someone?' Instead I say, 'Did he mention our other brother, Paul?'

'No. But I know about him.'

'You do?'

'I am a detective. It is my job.' He smiles.

I pause. 'Is there anything you can tell me about him, about Peter, I mean?'

The detective says nothing for a while. Then he shrugs and says, 'I am sorry. He was a client, a good one. But I did not know him well. We did not talk about anything other than the case. In fact, we did not speak very often at all. My instructions did not vary much. He always paid his bills on time. There was no need to speak.'

'And you won't tell me why he kept me under surveillance for years.'

He smiles and shrugs. 'He never said.'

'And my father?'

'I remember him.'

'Good.'

'Not well. It was a long time ago – 1995, I think. He was embarrassed to be employing me. I remember when he first came to see me. It took some time to get out of him what he wanted.'

I say nothing.

'I have no children. Sometimes it is better that way.' The detective leans back in his chair.

I stand up.

'You were not at the funeral. Your father's, I mean.'

'I was in England.'

The detective smiles. I want to be away from this place. I turn to go.

'Perhaps your brother wants you to figure it out. Isn't that what you have to do now? To work out his game?'

'Why do you use the present tense?'

The detective laughs. 'It is a manner of speaking. You say your brother is dead, but to you he seems more alive than ever.'

I do not like this man. I stand up and begin to walk out.

When I am at the door, he calls out. 'You look so much like him. You could be his twin. It is quite remarkable.'

I don't know what to say to that. I nod, and leave.

At the bottom of the stairs, there is a door which has a pane of glass at eye level. I can see my reflection in it. The mole on my cheek, the hairline, the scar on my chin. A thought goes through my head as I look at myself. You are not him. You are as innocent as a child.

I am about halfway down the drive when I sense something wrong. I coast to a stop. I cannot put my finger on it at first. I get out of the car and look at the house. And then I see it. The front door is open. Not much, just an inch or two, but open nonetheless. I remember locking it. I feel in my pocket for the key. It is not there, but I am sure I took it from the lock.

I stand looking at the house, watching the door, the windows, waiting for movement.

There is a breeze. It is warm. It comes from the mountains, this wind, from a place far away from here. I could turn the car around. I could drive towards those mountains, drive and drive, the air growing hotter around me. Eventually, on a white plain, shimmering with heat, I see a tree. I point the car at it and under the tree – very large for the desert – the car runs out of petrol and comes to a stop. I stay there, stay in the car and wait for the heat to rise. Smoke first, then the car bursts into flames. Me, too. Blue flames rising from my skin, my hair. There is no pain. I close my eyes as the flames grow higher.

He is in the house – Peter. I am not sure how I know. Who else would it be? It has been building for some time. Do I believe he is not dead? It is a question that is beginning to make less sense to me. He is in there, waiting. This is the thought that comes upon me. I let it take over.

I do not turn the car around, do not drive off. I cannot. I close the car door and walk the rest of the way to the front door.

I stand outside, listening. I can hear only the wind. I push the door further open, step inside and close it quietly behind me. The key is in the lock on the inside of the door. I take it out and put it in my pocket. Again I listen. Minutes pass. The house is quiet, so quiet it is as if I have stepped into a void.

Then I do hear something. A footstep, just one. I move towards the stairs, stop. The sound again. The noise could be the house shifting, settling in the wind. Houses make noises. I take the stairs, one at a time. On the landing I look up to the corridor above and wait again. I see nothing. And then a different noise – singing. A child's voice, faint. I hear it, but as soon as I do it is gone again. Now I take the stairs two at a time. I run into each room, starting with the main bedroom. Each room is bright, filled with sunlight but nothing more.

I come to the last bedroom, the one with the room under the eaves. There is nothing in the bedroom. But I stand in front of the door to the attic room. It is still closed. I have not been in here yet. Not this time.

I draw the bolt back. I can hear only my own breathing now. The voice has not come back. My breathing is quick. I push the door open. The room is dark, blacker than I remember.

'Hello?' My voice sounds strange, unreal. I think for a moment it has come not from me but from the blackness in the corners of the space that I cannot see. I wait for my eyes to adjust. There is no answer. A slight echo perhaps. I step towards the door and freeze. The song again, but from outside this time. I run to the window which looks out to the side of the property. I cannot see anything at first, but I open the window and stick my head out. Peering round towards the back of the house, I see something then. There, standing in the middle of the lawn, a boy. He is looking away from the house, towards the bush. He is too far away to see clearly and the window is at the wrong angle. I have to lean far out of the window and strain my neck to see him. The boy stands there. He is too far away to have made that noise, but I know it comes from him. Though it seems to start in my head, I know it is from that boy. I know the tune, though I cannot place it. The boy is still, his back to me.

I feel myself grow cold. I remember the open door behind me. I picture something emerging from it. Something dark, emerging into the light of the room, tiptoeing up to me crouched at the window.

Not just something. Peter. A sight more terrifying than anything I could imagine.

I turn. There is nothing. Still the cold.

I look out of the window again. The boy is gone. But then I look down and there he is, standing at the side of the house, pressed against the bricks. I pulled my head inside for less than a second. Or was it longer? It might have been longer. Have I been standing here for minutes, lost in a dream, before waking again?

I watch the boy and slowly he turns his head, turns towards me and looks up and meets my gaze. His eyes are black. The blackest things I have seen. The sun, perhaps, is in my eyes, and has burnt a patch in my vision so that when I look at this child I see only blackness.

I pull my head inside and lean against the wall. It is cold in here. I edge along the wall, my face to it, so I cannot see behind me. I do not want to look.

The boy's face. The face from the photograph.

I can still hear the nursery rhyme. Fly away, Peter.

Once out of the room, I run down the stairs and through the front door and round the corner of the house where I saw the boy, but he has gone. I circle the house and turn around and search the other way but it is all light here, no shadows, and I cannot see him.

The front door has closed behind me. I drop the keys as I take them out of my pocket, and when I bend down to pick them up, I see him again. Right next to me. I can see his feet, his calves, his knees. Just that. If I move quickly, lunge at him, I could catch him. I do not move. The legs do not move either. On his right knee there is a cut. It is healing, but it is deep. When it was cut, I could see bone.

He is barefoot. I stay bent to the ground, next to him, my skin tingling, expecting a touch. The boy's feet have the brown skin of a child who spends all day in the sun. The nails are bitten. He moves a toe. No, he is trembling. He cannot help it. He is afraid. Scared to death – of what I do not know. It is I who should be fearful. I dare not look at him, dare not move at all.

I smell it before I see it – urine. His leg darkens, urine washing away dust. A puddle forms around his toes.

Then I move. Just a fraction. But the boy moves too. I see his feet swivel and legs begin to turn. I see footprints in the dust next to me. The boy's feet still damp. They leave prints but in the sun, the wind, they vanish quickly. I try to move more quickly, to stand up at least, but I cannot. There is a force holding me back, pressing down on me. I watch the legs disappear. By the time I stand, the boy is disappearing around the side of the house. I look back and the prints are gone, the dust undisturbed.

I follow. I walk away from the walls so I cannot be surprised by him hiding around a corner. I see him in the distance. He has moved very quickly. I see him stop and turn around. He looks back, but not at me, at a spot to the left of where I stand and higher up. I turn around.

And then, in the dusk, I see Peter. It is him, there is no doubt. I do not know what to make of it except that I know it is him. He is inside, standing at a window on the second floor in one of the bedrooms, my bedroom. He stands there and his figure is white and though I can barely see him, I can see he is looking at the boy too.

The look on his face. It keeps me here, in front of the wall, keeps me here as surely as if there were stakes through my arms and legs. I watch, watch him watching the boy, the wall pressing into my skull, until the room darkens and he fades with the last of the light.

9

Standing there, pinned to the wall, I go through how this could happen, if it has happened. I think back to what I saw when I arrived at the house for the first time. I knocked on the door and received no reply. I walked around the house and found the kitchen door open. I walked through each room, but somehow I knew where to look: his bedroom that he had as a child. Being the eldest, he got the one with the extra room in the eaves. We played in there sometimes. I remember a model railway, miniature trees, houses.

I walked into the bedroom, and then opened the door to the second room and there was Peter, floating in the air before me. And then – it may have been minutes or even days – the police arrived.

I find myself going through scenarios. Mirrors, cameras. Was I watching a screen and recorded events playing out in front of me? Were the police officers who arrived in on the plan? Why would he do this, construct this charade? It makes no sense. Perhaps it was the only way he could think of to convince me to stay, his guilt blinding him to the absurdity.

The vision of him at the window is now more real to me than the memory of my brother flying for the second and last time in his life.

I move away from the wall, but I do not remember moving, do not remember going inside. There is a time – how long I do not know – that is simply gone.

If I think of this time that is gone, I find myself imagining being in the bungalow, watching the screen, watching a man running through rooms, aimlessly, chasing ghosts.

It is night-time and I am in bed. The house is quiet. I can sense he is not here. I get out of bed and go through the other rooms on the floor. In each, I stop to look around and open the cupboards. There is nothing inside. In the room before the main bedroom, after I have closed the cupboard, I look out of the window, the one that faces the road. I am about to turn away from the window when I see, out there on the road, leaning against a tree, a man. At least, the shape of a man. That is what it seems to be. It is hard to tell. If I look straight at it, it seems not to be there. Out of the corner of my eye I can see the shifting of black against the grey tree trunk. I stand in the dark, wondering if I can be seen too, wondering if I should go out there, check it is what I think it is. I don't think I can be seen. I am not standing in the light. I watch him. After a while the movement stops.

I go back to bed but do not sleep. Every hour or so, I check the window. Every time the shape remains. When it starts to get light, I look again and there is nothing there.

Later I am asleep. I know I am asleep because I have a dream. In the dream I am lying in bed. The moon picks out my shape. I have left the curtains open. In the doorway, and this is how I know it is a dream, stands a man. At least I think it is a man. He has no face. Where his mouth and eyes should be there is only shadow. The darkness seems to come from him. At his sides, fingers curl. They are long, too long. They curl back on themselves, the fingernails inches long.

Though it is a dream, I have a sense of time. Or that is how it seems. The man is there for hours, watching me sleep. When I wake, it is light and he has disappeared.

A photograph is next to the bed. I pick it up. Peter and Paul laugh together in the foreground. I can hear the laughter through the years. It echoes through the empty house. They are almost the same height. Behind Peter's laughter could there have been jealousy? He might have believed his younger brother would one day be taller, stronger than him. Somehow I find the thought reassuring, as if it is something to hold on to. I look at myself, sullen in the background – or, not sullen, simply caught at the wrong moment. I cannot remember, too long ago to remember.

The next night, I go back to the window to see if Peter is there in the road again. I will call him Peter. It is too dark to see. I turn off all the lights in the house and stand at the window, waiting. I stare at the spot where I saw something and I stare for so long I cannot tell whether what I see this time is there or is a memory of the night before.

I take an axe from the garage and go out of the kitchen door. At the corner of the house, I peer round at the trees lining the road. I cannot see the place where Peter was standing from here. I move quickly away from the house towards the fence at the side of the property. Halfway is a tree. I hide behind it. From here I can make out a head. It does not seem to be looking this way. Once at the fence, I walk alongside it towards the road. It is darker here because of the hedge in the neighbour's garden. I climb over the fence and walk along the verge, keeping to the shadows. The head peers out from the tree, framed against the sky.

I step closer. It does not move and I slip behind the tree. We stand on opposite sides of it. Me and the man on whom all this, all that has passed, rests. I wait, take a breath. And then it just comes out. I do not plan it and have done it before I realise I am doing it. Instead of showing myself to him, surprising him, taking the axe to him and ending it – for what would I lose by killing a man who is already dead, a man who is himself a killer – I speak.

'John.' I say my own name. It puzzles me. I look at the ground, at my feet, at the axe in my hands. It floors me, this word. I sink to my knees.

Then it comes to me – what I meant to say, or, I make it up, something that makes sense. I say again, my voice soft, 'It is me, John.' But I know he is no longer there. I feel the withdrawing, the absence of him.

I wake up on the couch in the larger of the two houses. It is dark. Still dark or dark again, I do not know. Then I realise there is something covering my face. A cloth. I fling it off and sit upright. There is no one else in the room. My face is damp, the cloth wet.

I listen. The darkness was not only from the cloth. It is night. I am losing track of time.

The room has not changed. The chair faces the same way out into the garden. The photos are next to it. The curtains have not been touched; everything is in its place from what I can see. From the rooms above, a sound. Not a sound, a presence. I close my eyes, but hear nothing, not even the wind outside. This is wrong. I should be able to hear that, hear something at least. I open my eyes a fraction. You could not tell, if you looked at me, that they are open. My eyes are slits, the world dark.

Peter stands in front of me.

He stands in front of me, arms at his sides, just two metres away. I stay seated on the couch and he standing in front of me. He looks like me, a slightly older, thinner me.

He moves his lips. It is like I am drugged, half asleep. I still cannot hear. I strain to catch his words, but I cannot. I cannot move either or he will know I have seen him.

I try to read his lips. 'Look at me, John,' he is saying.

I am looking. I am looking, but tell me what you want me to see. I think this but do not say it.

Then he turns and disappears into the dark. Slowly I begin to hear again as the house comes back to life. A sort of life. It starts with the wind outside, then the creaking of the wood, the bricks, the tiles. Then the voices – lots of them. I can distinguish different voices at first. It does not bother me that I recognise them: my father's, mother's, the other boys'. They mix into one another, speak over each other, louder and louder. They sound like flies. I cannot hear again, this time for the noise. The voices grow louder and louder and I close my eyes and lie back on the couch. I turn to the back of the couch and place my hands over my ears.

He is back. I cannot explain it. I cannot explain where he is when I cannot see him, how he manages to live here or close by without leaving more signs. He leaves some traces: a familiar smell, photographs in different places from where I've left them, a shadow down the corridor that disappears when I approach.

His death a lie, like so much else with him.

I get up later. I walk through the house but he does not show himself. I do not go into the room under the eaves. Though I saw nothing earlier, he may be in there, living in a corner like a hermit, blanket on the floor, an open tin, a small fire, the rest of his belongings stashed in a gap between the roof and walls. I sniff the air for smoke.

I take a shower for the first time in days. I stand under the water and watch it run off me. I keep my eyes open, watching, even letting the soap run over them.

I stare at myself in the mirror. My shoulders slump, I look older, I've lost weight. I shave off my beard. After I have dressed, I lie down on the bed. Though I have only just woken, I sleep again.

When I wake, I remember having seen Peter standing over me, reaching out a hand and brushing away a strand of hair. I wipe my hand over my face. It is like a spider has crawled over it.

I try to put these thoughts to one side, to step outside of them. I think of Rachel. I want to pick up the phone, hear her voice.

I close my eyes and try to picture her. Dark blonde hair. The down at the back of her neck. Grey eyes. A freckle on her cheek. The scar just below her knee, like mine. A cycling accident when she was twelve. Or did she trip on that hill in the Chilterns? I am beginning to question everything. I see her in Battersea Park, lying under a tree in the long grass, one foot flat on the grass, the other leg straight. Her arm behind her head. I see these things. I try to see into her face, try to get her to look at me, try to get closer to her. I see parts of her. The whole of her is somewhere else, just out of my gaze.

I open my eyes and there is the boy. He stands out on the lawn in the bright sunshine. He looks into the house, straight at me.

I need to keep him away. He sends a chill through me, the way he looks at me. He knows everything. A boy should not know that much.

Though I fear this apparition, at the same time I want to go to him, to hold him, to cup his blond head in my hand.

I wonder, looking out at him, if that is mist I can see. It

looks like mist rising from him, water evaporating in the sun. It comes off him, floats around him, his edges blurred. I close my eyes again and see – imagine I see – the boy coming closer, moving haltingly. The right leg leads, the left coming to meet it. I had a limp for a few days after the accident. I remember this now. When he moves his leg forward, his head dips. Like a dog. I am about to be torn apart. He is so small, a tiny child almost swallowed by the sun and the dust. He, the dog-boy, comes to the window, places his face against the glass. I do not move. He moves his lips, but no sound comes out. They make a shape and the lips form words. The words seem like 'Help me'.

I knew the boy I saw was not just some child wandering onto an abandoned property in search of adventure. I knew it, but it is a hard thing to say.

I look at the photograph again. To check, I tell myself. I look at the third figure in the background, then back out into the garden at the boy. They are the same. Even to the extent their colours are faded, they are the same. I have to accept – somehow, I do not know how – the child is me.

Time passes. I am gone. It is like I am an old man. I smell decay. It comes off me, wafts up through the roof, sifting into each room. My hands are wrinkled, dried out. And, through all this, outside in the garden, looking in at the window, I see the boy, this thing I cannot think of as a boy any more. He stares in at me, stares through me. I am stranded here in an unknown time, a forgotten place. All that is left is for the creature to find a way in. It is coming – it takes a step forward, a quick step, a lowering of the shoulders, a mock charge. The world is silent.

And now, they are all there. I cannot pinpoint the moment they arrive. It seems natural that they should be there. The man, the woman, the three children: my family. Me at the end, eyes poked out. Black holes. What have you seen? I have my back half-turned to my family. I cower. There is no other word for it. I flinch at the sight of them.

They stare at me through the window. My father – he stands at the window, arms at his sides, staring in at me and there is nothing to stop him coming in, nothing to stop any of them coming in. My mother at his side: her hair is grey. It was never grey. They stare through the window and I wait for them, wait for them to step through it. A film of water. I force myself to look away, away and up at the ceiling, the blankness there. I move my arms so they hang from the chair. I try to relax my breathing.

And then I feel it.

Hair beneath my fingers.

I cannot move them.

The touch is light. It could be nothing. A breeze. Yet, it is not nothing.

I look outside and the smallest child has gone. Only four of them now. They look in at me, at us.

A head shifts beneath my fingers. I feel the soft touch of a scalp. I want to move my fingers, to stroke the head of the child beneath them – give him and me some comfort in our fear – but I cannot move. I cannot give this. Not to him. I cannot give him what he wants.

I am frightened, more frightened than I have ever been in my life. Not of this. Not this, this thing beneath my fingers, or them out there. Of something I cannot name.

The boy does not move either. Fractionally maybe, but perhaps it is just his hair moving in the breeze.

He is just a boy, a child. Of course he won't make the first move. Of course it is not up to him.

I sit here, my eyes closed, my face wet. I make no sound. Through me flows everything: Paul, Peter, my mother and father, Rachel.

I sit here until – and I do not know when it changes, I have no awareness of the day ending – it is dark and the boy has gone and when I look, everyone else has gone too and the garden is empty.

I wander the house, touching the walls, turning off every light, leaving the house in darkness. I climb the stairs and go to the attic entrance. Outside I call softly, 'Are you in there?' I feel awkward doing so. 'Peter?'

'Leave him alone. Can you hear me? Leave the boy alone. He does not understand, did not understand.' I do not plan the words. They just come.

I stand outside the door with my hand on it. Eventually I push it open and step inside. There is a smell in the air, a lingering scent. I recognise it but cannot place it. My neck tingles. I have the torch I found in the bedroom with me. It casts a dim light. I shine it around the room but there is no one else there.

In the room is a table and one chair. There are slits of light in the roof. A house in need of repair. I sniff the air again, trying to place the smell, like damp earth. Like a man has been living here, cooped up for weeks. He has planned this well, drawn me in, painted the backgrounds, erected the sets. Now I sit here in the house, a captive audience, and he shows me mirages – each wall, each surface, a white sheet. On it he projects images. When I reach for them, they disappear, like smoke. He sits in a dark room – I can see him – watching me, shadowing me.

A thought comes to me. The house next door. Though before I did not believe he was staying there, perhaps now that I have discovered him, he has moved back to safer ground. I go to the window from which I can see the house. The shutter sways in the breeze.

I run down the road and then up the drive of the neighbouring property. I have the axe in my hand. I run over thorns in my bare feet, but I barely notice. I ignore the shutter and instead go round to the porch entrance. Even from a few metres off, I can see the door is open. I cannot remember whether I left it open the last time I was here. I stand outside it.

'I know you are in there.'

There is no answer.

'I want to talk to you, just talk. Please.' Again, it is like someone is speaking for me.

I step inside. There is the television. On the floor next to the laptop is a heap of DVDs. Many have been opened, the wrappers scattered around the room. I know I have opened some of them, but all of them? I do not know.

I walk through the rest of the house, flinging open doors and cupboards. He is not here.

The boy. The thought frightens me. I run back up to the road. I am not thinking clearly. I should have just gone through the hole in the fence. It is like I am being led.

As soon as I see the house, I know why. There is a light on. One of the upstairs bedrooms. I stand looking, then move quickly behind the tree. I retrace my movements. I went through the whole house turning off the lights. It is impossible I missed one. The doors to the bedrooms are all open – I would have noticed. I wait. Then movement, a figure shifting in front of the yellow light. The light spreads out behind him. In the centre, just darkness, the deepest black I can imagine. A figure standing in front of the light, now swaying, drifting in front of it, back and forth, back and forth. A moth, a lamp.

I cannot tell if the figure is looking at me or out the other way.

Suddenly it is dawn. I have not moved. It is dawn and there is someone at the window. I can see this very clearly, too clearly. There is someone there. The boy again, but older this time. A boy of twelve.

And I remember what I was watching when I was standing there, unable to sleep, not wanting to stay in bed. I remember hearing noises in the house, my father and mother shouting my name, and Peter's, and footsteps past my room and down the stairs and then a car starting and I knew who it was. Of course I knew. I watched her drive up the road, and standing here all that time later I watch the car again. There she is inside it, and all I want to do now, and then, especially then, because I knew, somehow I knew what was coming, was to run to her and put myself in front of the car and not move. She would have to drive through me. Kill me, kill me instead. She would have to drive through me to go and do what she was going to do.

But I was frozen. I am frozen.

It took her fourteen hours. She left at night and it was midday when she went off the road. What was she doing for all that time? Did she sit by the side of the road watching the sun rise in her rearview mirror, hands clenched around the steering wheel?

You were wrong, Dad. You were wrong about this and other things too. So many things. Not too young to know at all.

I drop to my haunches at the base of the tree. It is dark again. With the tip of the axe I scrape at the bark.

I hear a voice when I get inside, a man's voice. It comes from the lounge. I walk softly along the corridor. The voice speaks, then silence, then speaks again. A conversation on a phone. Or a man talking to himself.

I have left the axe behind. I do not remember putting it down. What is the voice saying? It is the same phrase over and over, but I cannot make it out. It sounds like 'Flying and could not stop'. Heard so many times, it loses its meaning. It could be anything. Static from a distant galaxy.

I peer around the doorway. In the moonlight, standing in the corner of the room, his back towards me, my brother. I take a step back. His head jerks downwards but does not turn and I have not made a sound.

His head. It jerked and was pulled and it was like he was pulled up into the air, pulled by his neck. Do not fear the hanged man.

Another step back and I am out of sight. I close my eyes slowly so it is like a curtain being drawn.

I hear the door to the garden open. I look into the room again. He has gone. I step into the room and face the wall just like him. I stand where he stood, in his footprints if I could see them. The paint on the wall in front of me seems to shine. In it I think I can see myself, a grey figure melted into the wall. 'I was flying,' I say to myself.

I look up at the ceiling. I am looking for him there. It pains me to say it.

I am talking now. The words lost, the tone flat. I talk and the words are lost and I see myself come into the room and look at the figure talking. Time loops back on itself and I am lost too.

Another voice, a child's this time. Faint, from upstairs. I go to stand in the corridor. It is muffled. I walk up the stairs and into the bedroom at the end of the corridor. Out of the window I see the branches of the tree being blown by the wind. That could be the noise. Wind blowing through cracks in the house. I open the door that leads to the attic. It is black inside. I step into the room. It smells in here, that smell when something has died – some creature that crawled into a far corner and starved to death. I wait for my eyes to adjust. There are pinpricks of light, as if the roof has stars. I see the outline of a table and hanging over it a rope tied to a roof beam. It moves. I think I imagine it. I stare at it for some time but I cannot decide if it is moving or not. Perhaps it is me swaying from side to side and the rope is still. Or the wind blowing through the roof. Or perhaps the rope is not there at all, not this time, and I am imagining it, bringing the past alive again. I lift my eyes and in the corner something black, darker than the surrounds.

I go up to it. A man's coat hanging from a hook. Do I remember this from before? From just hours ago? Or was it days. I have lost track.

A smell comes from it. The sight of it, the smell of it makes me want to retch.

The child's voice again. Not the wind. I strain to hear. It is quiet, as if far away. But I know it is not. It is coming from the coat, from behind it.

I go closer to it. I strain to make out what the voice is saying, but the words are like a foreign language to me. A nursery rhyme, the voice lilting.

I wish I had not come here. Not just this room, not just this house, this city, this country, this place that no longer knows me, that I can no longer call home. I regret the whole thing. The letters, the separation, the stories told: the whole thing, back to this very house where it all began. The true story, approaching me now from the end of a darkened tunnel, will break everything, everything that is not already lost.

I reach out and touch the coat. It is wet. Drops from it

fall to the floor. The stink hits me again. I know what it is now, the smell. The smell Peter left behind. Meat warming in a butcher's store after the electricity has failed.

The voice stops. I take the coat by the lapel and move it slowly to one side. Nothing. I let it fall back. I take a step backwards, then another. The voice again, louder, more insistent, angry even. The words.

I look behind me and through the door into the black of the outer room. Nothing. I rub my fingers together. They're wet – from the coat. I sniff my fingers: urine. I look down. At my feet, spreading out from beneath the coat, a puddle. I back away. At the doorway I stop again. I hear the words – different words.

'You're a liar, John Hyde. You're a liar, John Hyde.'

It is soft but it echoes around the room and sets my ears ringing. I want to put my hands over my ears and close my eyes and run from there. But there, sticking out from under the coat, the bare white feet of a child, urine running over his ankles onto the floor.

I do not run from this. I could not anyway. I could leave the room, the house, the country. I could return to Rachel, if she would have me, which I doubt; return to my job or find a new one. I could get on a plane and retreat over the African continent. But if I do that, I know if I do that, if I were to board the plane, take my seat, watch a movie, I know that when the lights went out all I would have to do is turn my head and there, a few rows back, sitting quietly in the dark, the child, staring at me, staring, unblinking, at me.

I sit down, my back against the wall. I watch the feet of the boy – my feet. I watch as the toes wriggle.

I see the coat move. I want the boy to come out. And yet I don't want him to come out – I dread it. Pearls for eyes. The tongue of a snake.

I try to talk. I try to say something. Anything. I take a breath, form my lips, but I cannot do it. I don't know what to say.

Outside the wind stops. The house is silent.

10

There are four of us in the car: me, Peter, and in the front our mother and father. I reach into the pocket of the seat in front of me and pull out a toy, an Action Man. Paul's. He left it there when we went down to the river valley.

Peter is out of the hospital. He was only kept in for two nights.

We're driving back from the police station. I am surprised we are all going home. I thought they would keep at least some of us behind. Peter, my father, me.

But they let us all go. They listened and asked questions, then let us go.

We're driving back home. I cannot look at Peter. I am turned to face the window. He is too. In the window I can see his reflection, and he mine. He watches me as I watch him. Whichever way I turn, I feel his eyes on me. I want to get out of the car. I imagine doing this. I remember now. I remember wanting to get out of the car and walk along the road. Somehow I would find my way back to Barrydale and to the mountain pass and the pool, climb down to the rock pool where Paul died, sit on the rock and look at the water. The sun would be shining, warming the rocks. I would be alone, quiet, sitting on the spot where my father hauled first Peter's then Paul's body out, where my father hit Peter on the chest and put his mouth to his and hit him again and again, so much that I wanted him to stop, so much that I thought for a short while my father had killed him, hoped even. But his body convulsed and water dripped out of his mouth and Peter was not the one who died that day. I think water came out of his mouth. I could not see it. I was still on the ledge watching, hiding. It was too far away to see, to see that.

I would sit on the rock, sit very still and wait patiently, and after some time Paul would come out of the water, climb out and sit next to me in the sun, a half smile on his face. We would not talk. I would watch drops of water fall from his skin.

The journey is silent. Not one word is spoken. I remember that.

My father looks at me. The whole journey, he too keeps his eyes on me. Why are you looking at me? Stop looking at me. I haven't done anything.

As I stare out of the window, I remember the earlier journey, with my head out of the window, the wind in my face, the laughter from inside the car and the urge to scream, to scream loud enough to burst their eardrums as I felt the scorecard taken from my lap and then watched it float away.

We pull up to our house. This house. Everyone stays in

the car. No one moves. Perhaps a word from someone would have made things better. Not better, but provided a start from which things could get better.

And that might have stopped what was about to happen.

We listen to the ticking of the engine. My father, my mother, Peter. We sit as if we could stay there forever.

Calm – that is the wrong word, perhaps, but it is how I remember it – silent calm. My mother was not crying. My father did not speak. Neither did Peter. We were each still there, still at the river with Paul.

But we could not stay forever. It would have been better if we had. Perhaps the story would end there. A family sits in a car for eternity. They are calm following the death of a child. They sit and the days pass. One after the other they wither, shrivel up, the car rusts and what remains of them blows away in the wind.

My father moves first, my mother next, then Peter. I am still sitting in the car after they have all got out. My father has opened the boot and is carrying bags inside. I want to talk. All I want to do is talk. I want someone to say something, say anything, I want to hear someone else say something. But no one does.

Peter walks off to the garden. I watch my father watching Peter. He looks at Peter and doesn't call him back. I look at my father's face. I try to read it. I am only eight. I don't know what it means. It is blank to me. I try to remember what I was thinking at that point, what I was feeling towards them, towards Peter most of all. Did I hate him then? Did I blame him for what had happened? That too is gone. I remember the day it happened, at least I think I do, I remember other moments, but the things that I want to remember, the things that will reveal the truth to me, seem to be lost. Things are coming back, some of them – flashes. But I need to know more. I need to get inside it, relive it. I have seen only shadows, the leavings of moments.

I looked at my father, standing there in the drive, and I remember thinking, he is far away, far away from me.

Far away, but I felt he knew what I was thinking. He and I knew. He ran past the ledge and would have seen me, though he did not stop. Though my father was looking away, I felt him watching me – from his back, beneath his shirt, the stirrings of another. I can see the bones move in his back, eye sockets peering through skin. Stop looking at me.

My mother was already inside. She had left my father to lock up. I went to find her. I had not planned anything, not planned to say anything. I found her in Paul's bedroom and stood at the door. She had her back to me. I heard a soft noise, like a bird. She held something to her face: a shirt. I tiptoed up behind her. I was carrying a toy truck or car. No, Paul's Action Man. I was carrying it and I stood behind her and then dropped it. It made only the softest of sounds, but she jumped and half rose from the bed. The shirt, one of Paul's, slipped from her grasp as she rose. It was as if she had been pulled up like a puppet. Her arms swung out and I don't know if she meant to hit me. I think not. I don't know. She swung at me and her hand hit me on the ear. I felt dizzy and fell to the floor.

She screamed then. I had never heard her scream. She had not done that before, not since the first moments after Paul died. For days she had been quiet. But not any more.

She swung around, her arms in an arc. I fell to the floor and she crawled back, her back to the wall, again, as if she was being pulled, dragged by some force unseen. As if, rather, I was some kind of monster, the thing of nightmares.

I didn't do anything, Mommy. I didn't do anything.

She screamed, 'Get out. Get out. Get out.' I remember her saying it three times. I got out. I was crawling at first too, then running.

My father was standing outside. I don't know how long he had been there. He was standing still. I ran into him, bounced off him. He did not try to catch me, did not try to stop me. I bounced off him and ran to the top of the stairs. I looked back. He was still standing there, not looking at me but into the room. He had not moved. Daddy.

I walked down the stairs. I took them one at a time. Left foot first, then the right, onto the same step. I wanted to go back to them, both of them, one on either side of me, their arms around me, or even just touching me. I wanted to go back and I thought of going back with every step, but I did not. Each step took me further away. They could not have blamed me. They were upset. Their son had died in a tragic accident. That is what they would have thought. They were not there. They did not see what happened.

When I got to the bottom of the stairs, I ran barefoot into the garden, into the heat. I ran along the grass – I remember it crackling under my feet, burning. Through the burning grass I ran, and I can see myself now, as if standing on the roof of the house. I watch myself run away, growing ever smaller, until my edges, the boy's edges, start to break up and he disappears into the heat haze, into the dust, into the bush, to find Peter. To find Peter, and – though I do not think I knew it then, and was not planning it – to begin the story.

I leave the attic, crawling out of the door, standing up only when I am out of the room. I walk down the corridor. From one of the rooms I hear laughter. I put my ear to the wall but do not go into the room. The laughter does not get any louder. Instead, all I hear is a hum from my ear against the wall – the sound of an ocean.

In another room there is crying. The voices of children, men, women. Or, just one man, one woman.

'Paul?' I whisper it.

From the main bedroom I hear sobbing. I run towards this. I think it will be the same as the laughter, though. Just the sound of the house, the house shifting in time. But it is not. There is a woman sitting on the bed. She has her back to me. She has long, dark hair. She is wearing a nightdress and seems old. Not in years but in her bearing, the nightdress, the hairstyle. She is from another age. She sobs while sitting on the end of the bed.

I knock on the door – just once. She stops crying, goes completely still. Her back straightens and she begins to turn towards the door.

When I see her face, I can see it is my mother. She turns to me and looks straight at me. She can see me, across these years. Her eyes are focused on mine, not some point behind me. She has red eyes. She is holding a photograph. I can see the picture. It is me. Not my brothers, not the dead one – me. Why me? The picture is crumpled.

I take a step towards her and she is gone.

I go up to where she was sitting on the bed. I place my hand on the spot. It is cold. I look at the place, looking for an impression, a dent. There is nothing.

The axe is on the driveway. In the garage I find a crowbar and a saw.

I start ripping out the cupboards in the bedrooms. The wood splits, cracks, falls to the floor. I hack at them with the axe, prise off bits with the crowbar. I lift pieces, which I throw through the windows to the garden below. I am not wearing gloves and my hands start bleeding.

In some places, I expose raw plaster; in others, brick. I am covered in dust. What doesn't fit through the windows I carry downstairs and throw onto the lawn. I take the fittings from the lights and throw these out too.

I start on the room that was mine. There is a desk and drawers built in under the window and a cupboard on the opposite wall. A memory comes to me. I am lying in bed. I am ill, the same illness I had when Paul appeared to me. There is a noise in my ears. The sea. Constant waves of noise. Not the sea. Static from a radio, growing louder, then softer. The door opens. Someone, my mother, my father, looks in. They come into the room and walk up to the bed. They, too, seem to pulse, growing larger then smaller. Whoever it is stands next to the bed and does not sit down. I see lips move, but I hear nothing over the static. I try to work out from their expression what they are saying, but I cannot. I am lost, half asleep, feverish. When the door closes, I wake up properly. There is a wrenching in my gut as I remember then what happened just a few days before.

I lie there and I am covered in scabs. They crust over me. If I move, I crackle as if on fire.

There are words that come then. I cannot remember who says them, or if they are spoken at all. 'Where did you hurt yourself? How did you get those cuts?'

I try to summon up this memory. I try to reach back to the waking child's memory and take it, hold it for myself. But it slips away. What did he know?

In my old room, I do the desk first. I take the axe to the middle of it, then work on where it joins the walls. Then I take the doors off the cupboards. I carry these downstairs, then the shelves. The board at the back of the cupboards has come loose and when I push it I can see a space between it and the wall. Another memory: I hid something here. I cannot remember what. I put my hand in the space between cupboard and wall, but it doesn't fit. A child's hand could but not mine. I break the wood.

There is a piece of paper, yellowed with age. It is a picture, a drawing by a child. It shows mountains, a river. There are two stick figures in the picture. They have wings on their backs. Angels. They fly off the edge of the cliff, wings spread wide.

At the edge of the drawing, standing on the cliff watching them fly, is another child. He has his arms out, reaching for them, calling them back. A big red O where his mouth should be.

I work more quickly now, leaving large bits of broken furniture clinging to the walls. The carpets are filled with splinters. I am barefoot. I see bloody footprints. I do not feel any pain, though. I finish my bedroom, then move onto the others. In the main bedroom I leave just the bed. The sheet is covered in dust, splinters, flakes of paint. I leave Peter's old bedroom, the one with the door to the attic.

It takes me a day to do the upstairs. Downstairs it is only the kitchen and the lounge with its shelves to do. It takes another day to dismantle these. I do not eat, and drink only water. I sleep for just a few hours at a time.

I leave the bed during the night. I move into the passageway, aware of eyes high up on the walls, blinking down at me, recording everything they see.

I close my eyes and support myself on the wall with a hand. If I close them, perhaps he will come to me, perhaps he will appear. Peter – I can sense him, sense him wanting to be here.

The carpets are filled with blood. They ooze beneath my feet. I am shivering. The windows are open and a cold wind blows in. I take a step forward but my legs struggle to move.

They are weighed down. I am trying to walk on the bottom of a river bed, my feet tied to blocks of concrete.

I suck in water, cough, have to kneel. I kneel, then sit and try to steady my breathing. It is as if I am trying to lift the whole house with every rise of my chest.

I sit opposite the stairway. I concentrate on my breathing but it gets harder. Peter is on the stairs. He has drugged me. It is the only explanation. He has drugged me and I am paralysed. He is crawling up the stairs, one at a time, his face blue, eyes bulging. His body twitches, convulses as it crawls up the stairs. On his back – I can see it from this angle – the burnt image of a child's hand.

I would move. I would move, go back to bed, close the door, close my eyes. I would move and be free of this, be free of all this, but I cannot move because the boy is there too. He stands silent next to me, so close I could reach out and touch him – touch his hair, his pale skin. The blood comes from his leg. It runs like a river into the carpet.

The corridor is white, as if filled with mist, with smoke. In time it fades and I can move again. I rub my arms. They are covered in fine drops. They sit on the hairs of my arms. I am silver.

I take everything to the back garden, all the wood and broken furniture. I drag it piece by piece to the bottom of the garden, pulling it across the lawn. It sticks in places and rips up the grass. I breathe in the dust it creates. After a while there are furrows in the ground, lines drawn from the back door to a pile of broken furniture at the bottom of the garden. Looking down at the house from above, this is what would be seen: lines traced in sand and along one of them, an ant dragging a load. From it a plume of dust rises, drifts across the scene until it is lost in the expanse of sky.

There is a can of petrol in the garage. I pour it over the wood and in the dusk I watch as the flames catch. They leap higher than me. Sparks fly off in the wind.

I walk back to the house, go into the bathroom, and in the mirror I see my face black with dust and soot. My hair stands on end, blown by the wind, infused with smoke. I sit in the lounge facing the window, watching the glow in the distance. The flames flicker. In front of the orange light I see black shapes, figures that run in front of the flames. I focus hard on them, but they appear and disappear too quickly. They run into the flames, first blocking out the light, then exploding with a whiter flame and disappearing again.

I see Peter. I see him go outside, walk through the window and out into the garden. At the edge of the flames he waits, then walks into the centre of the inferno. He turns and faces the house. The flames begin to take, his hair burning with a white flame. He makes no expression of pain, though his face begins to shine, his skin to melt, features drooping. The cheeks first, the nose, the jawbone: they drop off and fall into the fire below. The man and his sins burn. In his place, when the fire is out, a raw stump of flesh, still bubbling, spitting in the smoke.

I am in the house, in the room under the eaves. I am standing a few metres away from the edge of a cliff. I can see it clearly. My eyes are open. There is a boy, Peter, standing on the edge. Near the edge. A little way back. To his right is just shadow, but I know Paul is there. Peter turns to look at me. Then Paul emerges out of the grey and he looks at me too. The wind blows their hair. Summer in South Africa. They are tanned, their hair brown but with streaks bleached by the sun.

I feel it before I see it. In the darkness, a few metres away, the boy stands. Me. He is turned away, his back towards me.

He is turned away, his head bowed, but I know he wants to do me harm, to be rid of me, to stop me remembering. I know him. I know all about him. Or I will. I am starting to remember everything.

I shuffle back. I can hear my own breathing. The boy turns and takes a quick step towards me. I feel my back against the wall now and move slowly along it towards the door. The boy sees what I am doing and takes another step closer.

He frightens me, this child, this boy-ghost. He frightens me, but, as before, I want to take him in my arms, cradle him, hold him, and though he would struggle, hold him until his thrashing dies down, until he understands, until he understands the great void of thirty years. Until I understand.

He opens his mouth. It is as if he is under water. Bubbles emerge from his mouth and a sound, a deep distorted moan. I try to make out the words, but I cannot. I reach the door and step through it.

I feel the boy come after me. I feel him step through the doorway into the room, but then stop. He wants to call out to me. I sense it. Not harm, perhaps he does not wish me harm. But he does not want me there, and it comes to the same thing.

I wait in the corridor, wait for him to talk. He does not. I sense him searching for the words, but they do not come.

I start on the carpets. I prise up the metal strip at the doorways, then pull the carpet up, loosening it from the tacks as I go. These I remove one by one or hammer flat. When I am done, I walk through the house, and without carpets and furniture it echoes around me. I walk, hear footsteps – my own – then I hear others, or think I do. I stop and they stop too, but momentarily behind mine. The echo perhaps.

When the echoes die down, I wipe the dust and grit from my eyes. I open all the windows to try to get rid of some of the dust, but more blows in. I can feel myself drying out: I can feel the dust, the dirt, come in through my eyes, mouth, ears, pores – almost feel it getting into my bloodstream, stemming the flow. Movement becomes difficult, and after a while – I feel for some time I would be sitting, unable to move, feeling only the pain of grit in my open eyes – I start to crumble. A breeze would get up, one coming through the gaps under the doorways, and slowly I would start to disappear. My features would be the first to go. Nose, eyes, lips: just an ever-widening hole where my mouth goes into my throat and into my gut. The soles of my feet would be the last. The little eddies blow around on the tiles before settling in the cracks between the walls and the floors, or are caught by a gust and blown off into the garden, through the trees, and deep into the heart of the country. The source of the lie scattered to the winds.

I think about burning the house down. I keep a few reminders – the photographs, the watch, the drawing – and move the car away from the blaze, pour petrol inside and around the house. There is little to burn now. The flames would singe the concrete, ruin the paint and plaster work, but not much more than that. Perhaps the windows would crack in the heat and the roof beams collapse, leaving the house open to the sky, the wind and the rain. In time, birds would nest in the attic and maybe then the last whiff of my dead family would be gone.

But I do not burn the house down. Instead, I will burn the rest of what I have ripped out of it. I drag it all to the bottom of the garden and place it on the pile of ash.

I look at the bush that surrounds me and remember what was here.

In the garage I find a torch and a spade. Back at the scrub line I shine the torch back and forth, searching for a way in.

There is a section with sparser growth. An old path. I have to move branches out of the way. I sever one with the end of the spade. A few metres in there is a clearing. A mound, with a thin layer of weeds and scrub growing on it, occupies all of the space. I climb onto it. A bird begins to call. It runs at me, calling all the time. I turn my back on it and start to dig. Apart from the first few centimetres, it is not earth that comes up. My spade starts to turn up paper, plastic bags, juice cartons. I try to work out how old they are, but I cannot see a sell-by date. I turn up old batteries, broken glass. My hands grow black. Much of the rubbish has been burnt. That is what we used to have to do. We took our rubbish to the end of the property and burnt it ourselves.

I dig at different points in the clearing. I turn the torch and dig where it shines. There is no method to it. I spend hours there. I am not sure what I am looking for. A sign, proof that we were here, something to bring them back. Properly back.

I straighten up and take a rest at one point. I look at where the beam shines. Across the mound and into the bush at the other side. I can see branches, leaves, shadows. The night is still. There is only the sound of my own rasping breathing and the steam from my breath. I will get cold if I stop for long. The beam flickers. I look at the torch and the beam shining into the bush. Where it lands moves away from me. Back again. Away. I fall to my hands and knees. I am in a cold sweat.

There is movement in the bush. At the edges of the torch-light, something moves – an animal, a man. I can sense it if not see it. I know I cannot fall. If I do, it will be on me. It will not mind the dirt on me, the stench of me.

But I feel myself falling. Not from where I kneel but from higher up. I feel myself falling towards the torchlight in the bush. I travel at great speed but still it seems to take forever.

The man – for that is what I have decided it is – moves behind me. I try to turn, try to grab the torch and swing it around. But I cannot reach it. When I reach out one arm, the other cannot support me and I fall into the rubbish.

He comes closer and I raise myself again. The blackness

closes further in. Now he is in front again – and behind. Like there is more than one of them. Four of them. I listen. I think I hear cackling from the bush. But there is nothing. Still only my breathing. I hold my breath. Now there is truly nothing.

I cannot hold it for long. I stumble to my feet. There is a cry, splitting the silence. My breathing is shallow now, and quick. I turn around and around, as if in a dance. Another cry. It is soft. I can't work out where it comes from. I wheel around and try to face these things in the dark.

And I grow angry now. I shout. It is not a word I shout. It comes from deep inside, the cry of a dead man. I shout at the bush and if I listened I would hear it echo. I remember thinking this: a voice in the dark, bouncing against the hollow walls of abandoned buildings in an abandoned city.

The noises stop. I shine my torch at the bush. I can see something there. I step towards it. A figure emerges out of the leaves, picked out by my torchlight. It is me, a child again. I am standing looking further into the bush. I approach, and as I get closer, I see what I am looking at. Peter. Twelve-year-old Peter.

I am taken back. This is where I came after the scene with my mother in Paul's room. Did I know I would find Peter here? Did I seek him out to tell him something, to talk to him? That part is lost.

I watch the boy – myself. I, he, has a camera in his hands. He puts it up to his face and presses the shutter. This is the photograph. The back of a boy hidden in the bush.

It is windy. The branches and leaves move back and forth.

Above this, another noise – sobbing, from Peter. It stops as the photograph is taken. He turns, slowly, to his youngest brother.

They do not speak for some time. Then Peter opens his mouth. 'Did you see what happened?' His tone is flat.

I do not answer. I watch the boy – me – carefully, but his lips do not move. Not yet.

Peter again. 'I don't remember what happened. The doctor said I might not ever remember.'

I am silent.

'The last thing I remember is leaving Mom and Dad on the rocks. They were setting out the picnic. Did you see what happened?' he asks a second time.

And then, I nod. I see myself nodding. It is a slight movement. As if my head was being buffeted by the wind. Perhaps it was that after all and I did not mean to nod. The wind gets in here too. Cuts through the bush, moves limbs, bodies, tosses words away, distorts them.

'Tell me. What did I do?'

The words hit me now as they must have done then. What did I do. I think those were the words. It is hard to tell.

I look at myself again, the eight-year-old me. His face, burnt by the sun and the wind from days spent playing outdoors, is blank. He is quiet. Then he opens his mouth. 'I saw.'

There is silence for some time, except for the wind. The hair of the boys is blown back and forth.

'Did I push him?'

It is dark, but I see my head move up and down. The wind again. Moving my head against my will. Peter sees it too, a small, almost imperceptible movement of the head. Yes, it was you. It was you. You and no one else.

Peter turns away. 'What did you see?' It is a whisper.

I do not answer. There is silence for some time.

He speaks again. 'I killed him.'

'I saw.' I cannot tell whether the sentence is ended or interrupted.

'Did I push him?'

I do not want to hear the answer. Me, the boy, twenty-eight years previously, about to answer yes, or simply nod again: that would be enough. Me, the adult, with that story stuck in him forever. A fish hook through a cheek and the flesh hardened over it.

Through branches I watch my brother crying and rocking back and forth on his heels. I know, knew then as a boy, I remember now, I knew then what I had done, what I have done. I knew what he had done too – Peter. I watch my brother, the camera forgotten now in my hands, and then I drop my eyes and look at my own feet and I know deep within the world has come to an end and that my chest holds more than it can bear.

I want to go to him now, but the distance between us is a chasm. Instead, I stand in the bush, staring at my feet, unable to look up, unwilling to look at what I've done.

I am a child again. I run from there. With the words hanging from the branches of the dried bush, I run. I crash back through the bush, run over the rubbish dump, and into the bush on the other side. I keep running, away from the house. I feel thorns in my feet, but I carry on. A branch hits me on the head, but I pick myself up and run blindly on and on until I crash into the fence at the bottom of the property. The barbed wire pierces me, clings to me. I try to pull myself off it, but it clings tighter. I feel my head spinning and the world begins to blacken.

And then the dogs come – the neighbour's, strays maybe. There are four of them, five, perhaps more. They run through the bush towards me. I hang on the fence. I see their eyes in the shade. They hurl themselves at the fence and I hear their barks and on my face I feel their breath and in my throat the foul smell of rotting meat. The tooth of one of them catches me and there is blood and I watch it drip into the dust. I remember this: I watch the blood, the silent fall, as if slowed down. I do not watch the dogs. I do not care about them.

I hang there, separated by wire from dogs that would kill me if they could. I wait. I will wait for them. The wire cannot hold forever.

I grow still, my breathing slows. I hang there, entangled, wondering how long I could stay here. How long it would take until I dried out, dried out so much the wind could lift me up and blow me away.

The boy is found later. Not by his father or mother, but by someone else. He cannot remember who. Perhaps a family friend arrived to lend support.

I think of me as other, as somehow not the same flesh and blood as I am now. Between him and me there is a break, a fissure.

I remember the cold. Not the weather – the coldness of bones. The boy wakes to footsteps behind him, then a voice. He cannot hear what it says. The dogs have gone.

The man picks the boy off the fence, eases him off. Meat off a butcher's spike. In truth he was not impaled, just pinned. The panic of an eight-year-old.

They return to the house, the boy in front, the man slightly behind. The boy looks at the ground, the man at the boy. I remember the back of my neck: ice-cold, as if gripped by an iron hand.

We step into the kitchen and my father is there, leaning over a sink, his hands on either side, head hanging down. He lifts it when he hears us come in. He looks at me, his boy. He looks at me and there is nothing on his face, a blankness that I, the man, had forgotten, but now remember. And it hits me again, the full force of this nothing.

The story that was out there could never be retold and never untold. The barbed wire, the dogs, the blankness on my father's face – these things pressed the story down, pressed them into me. Always there.

The man put his hand on the boy's back then, and walked him past his father. It was a tender touch but that made it worse – that it came from him, a man I did not know, or at least was not the man at the sink. I did not, could not, look at my father as I walked past, and I know my father did not look at me again. Not in a way that mattered. Though he did not know. He did not and would never know.

11

There is a drawing by Escher of a group of men – or one man, I cannot remember. One or many, they are dressed like monks, or soldiers. They walk up the stairs. Another group walks down the stairs, which surround a courtyard. They are trapped. One group forever going up, the other forever going down the stairs. As a boy, when I first saw it, I wondered what these men said to each other for the hundredth, the millionth time they saw each other. Perhaps they were too embarrassed. Perhaps they could not break the cycle they found themselves in because they were too afraid to stop.

I will break this cycle.

Perhaps not one or many, perhaps one and many. One man, many times.

I have not slept for days. I write it and I know it is a lie. I have woken up – come to – in places aware of what has gone before but not able to remember falling asleep. Does one ever remember falling asleep? The awareness of it depends on the absence of something to be aware of. I wake, too, in places I don't remember being in before I slept.

I am being watched, like I have been my whole life. I go into the house next door. I walk quickly and quietly to the bungalow, but I know I can be seen. It is no use trying to surprise the watcher. Two North Magnetic Poles. I know this.

I place the discs in the laptop, watch what has been recorded, watch for hours. I wait for him to come to me here, but he never does.

I watch the disc for signs of Peter. That is what I call him still, this doppelgänger. And I do see him. He creeps – that is the word – through the house. A few times I shout at him, call on him to come out, come and have this out, settle it once and for all, as if this was the Wild West.

Then he changes into me, or that is how it seems. Peter leaves one room, I appear in the next. He never comes close enough to come into contact, always careful enough to stay just out of my sight. I see myself running from room to room. I know what I am doing. If I am fast enough, sooner or later I will catch him.

And when I go next door to the larger house to sleep, he comes and stands over me while I do – I know it is not a dream. I see it the next day in the cameras. A man standing in the dark. I cannot make out what is in the bed, but I know I am there. I remember being there.

I know what I have to do.

The next night, I lie in bed and wait until I hear his footsteps come to the door and can feel him in the room, can feel the heat from him: flesh and blood.

I wait until he leaves the bedroom and then I get out of bed and walk to the corridor. I look down at the ground, not directly at him, for he would disappear if I did. I wait as he comes to the doorway of another room and stares down the passage at me. I picture his face. Fear, it may be fear. I stand there and lift my arm and tap at the wooden doorframe. A dramatic moment. I want him to feel this, to not pass through this moment with the indifference he has displayed all his life. I want him to know what's coming. I want him to know me, to know all he has done, all he has created.

In the light I walk through each room. I sniff the air. I can smell him, the stench of him. The smell in each room is strong. He has just been there. What you leave behind betrays you.

I wait again. I wait and the moonlight shifts over my form. I can see myself as if I stand in the doorway looking back at myself. The moonlight picks over my bones.

He comes to me. Killer. Liar. Shape-shifter.

He retreats down the corridor and disappears into the dark of the attic, but I don't follow him. I go downstairs and I throw a glass on the ground. I beat my fists against the walls. I run headlong into the windows in the lounge. I do this several times. My forehead hits the window frames and I am cut. My eyes are open all the time. I look out into the dark and wait for their approach, wait for them to come back to the window, to come inside. Do they know? Of course they know. They have known all along. They know what he did. What I did. Though it was never spoken of. Of course they knew. It was in my father's letter. They sensed it. My mother especially, I realise now. Just a child, they would have thought.

It was in my brother's letter too. The words that dragged me here in the first place. I did not believe them. I wanted to set him right, once and for all. I had blocked everything, changed the man that I am.

My family do not come. Now, it is me and the liar in the attic, we alone.

I wait downstairs. I stand at the foot of the stairwell and have to blink as the blood runs into my eyes. The blood stops and I stand, looking up, waiting for him to appear, but he does not. He stays hidden.

I lift the weight from my foot, as if to place it on the first stair, but I do not place it and I stay where I am and I do not go to him. I cannot do that, cannot confront him and all it means just yet.

He does not come back. He does not come back. Through all this time, I know he will come back. I know him as if he were myself.

The fourth night he comes back.

I wait for him, staring at the space next to where he is. I walk at him. He retreats. I walk at him and he retreats, and I force him back into the attic. As he steps inside, it goes quiet. Quiet again.

I look at him now, look straight at him for just a second, the light at the right angle, and a feeling of great weakness comes over me at the sight.

What do I do with him – the man in the eaves? I have no plan. What do I do? I will keep him here, the madman in the attic. I will keep him here and keep him here and keep him here, and so it will go on. He will starve; he will not hang himself or end it sooner. He will starve and in time his flesh will dry out. The tiles of the roof will fall off, the lining will go and he will be left to the wind, as he wanted. He will be scattered over these parts, to remain here forever with Mom, Dad, Paul – and with Peter. The boy on the wire will have his wish.

I see it all now and still I go through with it. I owe it to myself. I owe it to them.

12

John Hyde is on the floor of the attic room. It is cold. He shivers. The blood from the wounds on his head has crusted over and he feels if he moves he will tear his skull open.

He does not move. He lies there listening to the throbbing in his head. There are other noises too.

He hears movements in the house. He hears creaks, bangs. Some of the noises he thinks are human. Others he cannot tell what they are: the noises of the house settling, mice in the rafters, the wind through the cracks.

He hears a noise in the room behind him and stiffens. He does not get up. He cannot, in fact. It is as if he is glued to the floor. He hears the door open, and on his back, which faces the door, feels a breeze. He waits for a touch.

A footstep – just one – on the concrete.

He wonders how long it will take – for the noises to stop altogether; for him to be able to close his eyes and sleep peacefully.

Like a fish he opens and closes his mouth. His tongue sticks to the roof of his mouth and to his teeth. He tastes something. Metal. The head of a hammer in his mouth. He tries to spit, but there is nothing to spit. He tries to swallow, but there is nothing to swallow.

He shouts sometimes. There is no reply. He knows there will be no reply.

Through the night he drifts in and out of sleep. It grows lighter in the room as dawn comes. He waits for noise from the house. He tries to remember if he has heard anything since he woke up.

He feels he might be asleep again. He sees the boy, John. Standing under the eaves in the shadows, a boy, aged eight. He is dead, this boy, though not in the sense usually meant. The boy stands under the eaves in the shadows. Hyde cannot see his face, though the boy is turned to him. His face vanishes in the looking at it.

He wants to go away, this boy, he wants to leave here because he has made the place all that it is, all that it lacks. And he did. He went away for a long time. He went away a boy and returned a man and what he found is desert. Now he walks through where he remembers people, streets and buildings. Instead he finds sand dunes. Here and there a chimney pokes through. He uncovers a car. He skims the sand from the windscreen and peers in. Once his eyes get used to the gloom, he makes out a family. The father in the front seat, the mother next to him, three children further back in the gloom. He bangs on the windscreen. He wants to wake them up. He reaches in to them, but the sand begins to run through their mouths, their eyes, leaving just white bone. Hourglass people.

Hyde feels something coming from this boy – the coldness of years. The man on the floor retches.

Later he turns to the camera above the door. He laughs, mouths something at it. He pictures a man in front of the screen in the other house. He can only see himself.

Paul's death – he thinks he can remember it now. Everything that was buried, everything that changed over the years. That is why he is here, after all. To fill in the gaps. Perhaps once it was to hear his brother say 'Yes, John, you were right. I did it. Not you.' That is all he has ever wanted to hear, whether he knew it or not.

Dimly he imagines there might be more, more that he has not remembered. There is a moment missing. A hand on a child's back, the memory of the thought before the hand on the back. But he has seen enough.

He still feels he is being watched. He can feel eyes on him. He knows now it is the way he has felt for thirty years.

He lies awake through the night and into the day.

He breathes. Beneath his sweat-and-blood-stained shirt his chest rises and falls. Around him the house ticks in the heat of the sun. It is quiet here. A quiet place in the country.

He leans against the wall now. He sits on the floor and his

eyes are closed, but he does not sleep. He hears the outer door open.

Footsteps. They click over the concrete floor. Like the nails of a dog.

He opens his eyes and looks across the room. Opposite him, a man slouches against the wall. They stare at each other. When one moves, so does the other. Hyde looks at this figure, the greying hair, the sweat, the stubble, the drooped shoulders. He knows it now. The sight, sound, the presence of this man, the smell of him in this room, this man who killed Paul and has never paid for what he has done, not only in the killing but in the telling, in the not telling of it. He sits there, back against the wall, in the presence of the man who has brought the edifice of his life crashing down around him, and he cannot move. He has given up, given over to this, this realisation. He is beaten.

He hears crashes against the door. Blow after blow. They are coming. They are coming.

Hyde whispers to the man opposite, the sound almost drowned by the banging, 'What do you want?' It sounds mundane when he says it, the first words he has said for days. He watches the lips of the other move. He regrets talking.

'You.' The voice is so soft it might as well be in his head.

It is soft but it cuts through him – the sound of it, the lilt, the guttural South African voice underpinning a softer English accent. He knows every inch of this man. In every inch he sees himself, sees what has been, what might have been. He sees, staring back at him, a doppelgänger. He imagines this figure crawling up the wall and across the ceiling to hang, dripping, above him.

It runs out of him. Everything that he has, everything that he is, runs out of him, liquid, over the floor of an abandoned house in a forgotten corner of the world.

13

If there was a moment she knew she had made a mistake, an error of judgement, it was when she met John's brother in the park.

He said 'Hello' and she was still looking down at her laptop. It happened sometimes. A woman sitting alone attracts attention. But when she looked up at him, ready to smile and say thanks but no thanks, her mouth opened ready to speak and nothing came out.

It was her husband, but not him. There were only a few slight differences. The face was a few years older, more suntanned, though underneath the colour there was something missing. He was ill, though it was only much later she would realise this. He had a few more grey hairs than John, the jawline slightly different, the accent too. Though it was just one word he had said, it had a thicker South African tone to it. Her husband's accent was much less distinct. He had been in England many years and most people couldn't tell where he was from. Another disguise. She remembers now this thought she had at the time the man appeared in front of her.

She forgets how much time passed while she stared at him. It could not have been more than a few seconds.

He sat down. 'My name is Peter Hyde. I did not think you would have been told about me, and I can see I was right.'

The mistake was in not probing John's silence more than she did. She felt he would eventually tell her everything. It was too late for that now.

She does not remember saying more than a few words to her husband's brother. Though she knew there were holes in John's story, and knew she should have expected something like this, especially with all that had been going on, with John's obsession with the man, the ghost, she sometimes thought, watching their flat from the park, she remembers struggling to hear this man called Peter – what an ordinary name for someone like this – struggling to hear his story, focusing instead on the unreal vision in front of her.

He did not tell her everything. He introduced himself and explained that he and John had not seen or spoken to each other for eighteen years. He said something about it being because of an incident that got out of hand, that grew and grew because neither made a move to put a stop to it, and then it grew so much it could not be stopped. The power of a story – he used that phrase.

He was holding an envelope that she had not noticed before and now he slid it across the table. 'I would like you to give this to John. I am leaving now.' He got up from the table.

'You can give it to him yourself. He will be home soon. Please wait.'

'It can't be me. I have a plane to catch, and besides, I wanted to meet you. You seem to have made him happy.' He turned and walked off up the path.

'Wait.' There was so much she wanted to ask but her legs wouldn't move.

She looked at the envelope. It had John's name on it and their address.

Her husband was home early, a few seconds after her. For a moment she wondered if he had seen her in the park with Peter. He acted strangely as he walked through the door, did not say hello.

She gave him the letter, said something to him, but she can't remember what it was. She gave him the letter and went into the bedroom to pack a bag. She stayed in a hotel that night. He did not phone and she would not phone him. The next day she went to stay with her parents at their house near Amersham. After four days she sent him a text. There was no reply. Then she phoned him, but his phone was switched off.

A week later, she went back to the flat. He was not there. She knew he was not at work, though it was a weekday afternoon. One of the other suitcases had gone and his passport too. In the kitchen she recognised the same dirty plates from the day she'd walked out. He had left on the same day she had or very soon after.

She did not know where he had gone. Somehow she knew

he had gone after his brother, but had no idea where. There were stories of a childhood in Port Elizabeth, South Africa, but she had no address and did not even know if Peter would be in the same city, or even the same country.

It would not have been impossible to find out. She had a name, a birth date, a city. There are people who could find things out. For a moment she wondered if John had made other things up too: his surname, his date of birth.

But she knew she would not contact a detective. As much as she hated what had happened and the stories he had told, and as much as she wanted him to herself, she knew there was another story he had to unravel. This is how she thought of it. A story to unpick.

She finds the letter in her flat a few months later. One day the cleaner does not arrive and Rachel decides to clean the flat herself. In the bedroom she moves the bedside table to vacuum and sees the envelope between the table and the bed.

There are two letters in the envelope. She reads both. The longer one she reads three times. She returns the letters to the envelope and places the envelope in the drawer. She sits for a while. Just sits, does not move.

It is dark outside and a cold wind is blowing. She wraps her scarf around her. Battersea Park is closed but she climbs over the fence. There is no one around. From under the trees, she looks up at the flat. From here she can see the windows of two of the bedrooms and the lounge. This is where Peter stood, where he watched.

She has left the lights on. She waits, half expecting to see a shadow crossing the window panes, half expecting to see her husband move the blinds and peer out. There is nothing.

She closes her eyes and conjures up a memory of her husband. She sees his hands. She remembers him putting his hand on her thigh. They were sitting on the couch together. She reached out and put hers on top of his. It was a fraction of the size. She moved her fingers up towards his wrist, over the ridges of veins. She remembers the warmth of his hand under hers, the warmth on her leg. He had long fingers, always brown, no matter the time of year. Strong wrists. She liked holding his wrists, kissing the inside of them. She remembers the scar on his left, from the ring on his finger up to the middle of his hand. She remembers the streak of white on the brown hand. She traces a line on her own finger.

She asked him where he got it, that and the scars on his knee and chin. She asked many times. His answer was always the same. 'I fell when I was eight.' Just that.

Later, Rachel sits in front of her computer, an empty bottle of wine on the table. There is a credit card in her left hand and on the screen is an airline site. She leans back in the chair and looks out of the window. Rain and the branches of a tree beat against the window. There are no lights on in the room. The only light is from the screen and it makes her look grey. She has her hair pulled back. The light deepens the lines on her face. She looks out of the window at the rain, the leaves wiping against the glass.

She knows that if she got up from her chair, walked over to the window, put her face to it, she would see him. She would see him out there, standing beneath a tree, his collar pulled up against the rain. She would not be able to see his face but it would be him. John. He would be waiting for her to come down to join him.

And she knows she needs to find out. She knows she needs to find him again. She chose him after all. There is an ache in her. It is him, she knows this. She fights against the weakness she feels this represents, but she longs for the part of him she does not know.

The flight is full and she is wedged between two men. She sits with her arms folded for most of the journey and eats and drinks little. In a few hours she will land in Johannesburg, then will take a plane to Port Elizabeth. She has an address – the address written on one of the letters – and a satnav. But she has not spoken to John, does not know how to get hold of him and knows he might not be there, or even in the country. She begins to regret her decision to fly to South Africa, but there is no going back now.

She wonders what she will find when she gets to the address. She has a vision of him in a large house. Somehow he looks younger, less burdened. There is a pizza box on the floor, a movie on the TV. He is on the couch asleep. She sees a woman opening the door. From between her skirts a child peeps out. Not his, of course, but a family nonetheless. She wonders what she would do if this happened. Walk away.

It would be all she could do. She wonders why she can only picture him happy. She knows – is sure – this is not the case.

At the check-in desk, she realises she had booked her flight to Port Elizabeth for late afternoon. The wine, she thinks. She has hours to spare in Johannesburg airport. She sits in a coffee shop, her bag beside her, watching people. She finds she is looking for his face. He might as well be here as anywhere. She thinks about trying to change her flight. It would be easy: a midday, mid-week flight to Port Elizabeth, a place she knows is not a major centre, would not be full. But she waits. She thinks again about turning back.

When she found the letters, she wondered why he hadn't taken them with him. But, she reasoned, it was a difficult time. He probably packed in a hurry and the letters slipped down the side of the bed. Perhaps, she feels, he wanted her to find them, wanted her to know, unable to tell her himself.

She has brought the letters with her. She opens the first, dated March 2011, and reads it again.

1 March 2011

John

It may surprise you to hear from me after all this time. It may surprise you to realise I know your address, know where you live. You should not be surprised. You can get any sort of information if you pay the right people: your address, your place of work, your wife's name.

That may sound sinister. It is not meant to be. I do not wish to alarm you.

What I want is for you to come to Port Elizabeth. I am living in the house. You may know it was left to me when Dad died. I know you know about that too.

I realise we have not spoken since 1993. There is this thing between us. I would like to talk about it – once and for all. Clear the air. You, no doubt, will be curious.

You do not have to reply to this. Just turn up. There will be a room waiting for you.

The truth is, John, and I debated whether or not to write this, I miss you. I miss both of you. You, though, most of all, because you are still alive.

Peter

Innisfree, Kragga Kamma Road, Port Elizabeth

She had not seen this letter, had not seen it arrive. Perhaps it had been sent to John's work. He did not tell her about it. She wonders what he had been thinking at the time; how he behaved the day he received the letter. She searches her memory for signs but there are none.

She takes out the second.

28 August 2011

Dear John

I will ask your wife to give you this letter. Though by the time you read this our meeting will have happened already, I can anticipate her reaction. It will be like she is seeing a ghost. You have not told her about me, have you? About any of us, I imagine.

You need not worry. I will not tell her our story. Of course, she may read this letter in which case your secret is out. Do you trust your wife not to read it, not to pry? The answer is obvious given you haven't told her about me.

Why is that, John? Why haven't you told anyone about me? About Paul? Have you lost trust in our story, in your story?

She is beautiful, your wife. Rachel. Perhaps I too could have had a wife like her. There is no time any more. I am past all that.

Dad died of a brain tumour. It was not a heart attack. I believe you were told it was a heart attack for some reason. Sorry to be blunt.

There is a letter from Dad for you in the drawer in the main bedroom. I have not opened it. I have no idea what it says. I was supposed to have posted it to you after his death. I am sure you will understand why I broke my promise to him.

Am I curious what is in the letter? Yes. Afraid? I will leave it to you to judge.

It seems like we have a habit of communicating through others. Dad's letter that I was supposed to send to you. This letter that I will send through Rachel. That was always the problem, wasn't it? Turning away from that which troubled us.

We put him through a lot, didn't we? Dad. It must have been hard for him. The silence between us and him on his own.

I have the same thing as Dad. It can run in families apparently, though they tell me I am unlucky.

Watching him go was horrible. We were never that close but we became closer in the end. Watching someone you love die makes you remember why you love them, what they have done for you.

Have you experienced the death of a loved one? Recently, I mean. I hope not. Why do I ask? I know you haven't.

He was in a lot of pain. They give you stuff for the pain and the medicine is probably more effective now, a decade later, but I will not go through what he did. It is decided. There is no one to look after me either, so I would be stuck in some shit hospital for ages, waiting to die, knowing that the nurses are waiting for the same thing. They need the bed after all. Other people need to die too, don't you know. Forgive the gallows humour.

The house will soon be yours, for what it's worth. Not very much, certainly not in your money. You might not even be able to sell it. The houses on both sides of me are empty and have been for some time. I own one of them, in fact. A bungalow bought as an investment many years ago. What a joke. No one can sell around here.

You might not even go to Port Elizabeth to try. You might decide to arrange it all from your flat in Battersea or your office in the city. An agent gets a call one day, next day a For Sale sign appears.

Battersea. It is a strange name. What does it mean?

Do you know? I don't know what the name of this place means either. Kragga Kamma. It sounds like someone clearing his throat. You would think I would have found out by now, wouldn't you? It shall remain meaningless.

You could give it away. Perhaps to a charity – a home for runaways, for lost souls. They might not want it, of course, once they know the history. One family. One child dead at a young age. Two suicides. A son who has cut off all contact and who still believes (I wonder, do you? Did you ever?) his brother is a killer.

They might think it is cursed. And who is to say otherwise? The house is not right, John. Not right at all. You will feel it when you come, if you come. A place can get overwhelmed by what went on there. Like Auschwitz, I imagine. I do not mean ghosts. Memories. The memories linger, even after there is no one to remember. No peace there.

I have some photographs of us. I will leave them in the house for you too. A photo taken of the three of us on the day Paul died, one from a few days later, a few others too.

I have cleared everything out of the house already. Most of it, anyway. But these things I will leave.

One of the photographs is of me. It is a bad photograph. It shows me in the bush, a tiny figure. It is old now so you can barely see me. The shadows are on my back and I have my back to the camera. It is dark.

Whether that is just the photograph not developing properly or whether it was dusk, I forget. Perhaps the shadows are from the moon. Funny how you remember some things and not others.

I do not remember the time of day but I remember what happened. We had just returned from hospital. The four of us in a silent journey. I walked across the lawn and into the bush and sat down and I know you followed me after a while. You took a photograph. Why, I don't know, but that's not what's important.

I asked you a question then. I should never have asked it. Do you remember?

I waited for you to give me the answer I wanted. An unreasonable ask, perhaps. You were only eight. I was just twelve, though. Still a child. You could have said anything, anything at all. Anything other than what you did say.

I could not remember what happened. For years I could not remember anything of it. It is not uncommon apparently. I could not remember, but I had a sense that the full story had not been told. They said we fell from a ledge and Paul hit his head. I was lucky. But that was not all there was to it. I knew there was more but I could not remember, and then you said what you said and that was the truth I had for most of the rest of my life.

I saw you. That is what you said. I saw you push him. The worst thing you could have said. The words made me retch. You made me believe you.

I was afraid of you. That was new. Afraid of my little brother. You held such power and I did not realise it.

Afraid you might tell. Afraid you were right. I had doubts, even then, about your story, but to hear you say it, well, you were my brother. You wouldn't lie, would you? Not about that.

Why didn't you tell? Sometimes I wish … not sometimes – I wish you had told. It would have been easier with your story in the open, your story exposed to the sun to either grow strong or wither and die.

For it is just that, isn't it? A story.

I will go through the story – let's call it that for now. Maybe it will help you. You have never let on that you do not believe your own story, not in the years we had together and not since, not to Rachel, not in an email or text sent while drunk, or in a careless conversation in a pub.

You see, I have been remembering. At least, I will admit, other stories have been sprouting in my thoughts – like weeds. That is what it is like.

I always start with the days before. I start with you and Paul and me. I tally things up. We found a dog on the road and poked it with a stick and made you get close to it and then gave you a fright by pretending it was moving. You cried your eyes out. In fact we were almost scared at how much you cried. In the car Paul threw your scorecard out the window. Were there other events? And then, on the day, on the way down to the river, I punched you. Just on the arm. You had fallen and cried out. I punched you on the arm. I was annoyed. I could relate to Paul. He was less than two years younger than me and strong for his age. We played together all the time, and, I am sorry to say it, but we felt you got in the way sometimes.

You slipped. I heard you cry. I came back for you. I saw that you had fallen but there was barely a scratch on you and you had held me up. Paul was going to get there before me now. I gave you a punch on the arm and then started to run down the path.

I heard you scream. You screamed at me, your frustrations of the previous few days overflowing (I imagine). I will kill you. Are those the right words? I do not remember them. Perhaps they were something else. Perhaps I am imagining all of this. Or, it is the cancer altering memories, deleting old ones, inserting new ones. How do I tell what is memory and what fiction? How do I tell if what has come back is the truth? You would know. Unless, by some big coincidence, you have what I have, you would know for certain. No matter what you've repressed, what you have changed, retelling yourself the story over and again, I believe you know, will know, will come to remember.

Paul was standing on the ledge. I pushed him to one side – a little. Before I saw how high we were. He did not fall.

We stood there for a moment and looked into the

water. It was a long way down. The water was that deep brown you get in the mountains, but clear. There were rocks below us, but beyond that the water was deep. We fancied we could see the bottom.

We were daring each other to jump. We knew we would have to jump far out and land feet first in the water. Perhaps even take a running jump. We took a step or two back.

We stood still, shoulders touching. There was a time in which we, and everything around us, were utterly quiet.

I heard something then, something rushing down a slope, or running, I didn't know what. An animal. Later, yes, I worked it out, worked out that it was you. But not then, not for years.

I do not remember how close you were. You might have been far back, not much closer than where I left you. Or you could have been right behind us, your breath at our necks.

The official version: Paul and I slipped and fell into the pool. I landed on my back and the fall stunned me. Our father, hearing a cry, came running. I was unconscious for just a minute. Paul, though, hit his head on a rock. The angle and the length of the fall meant that he died instantly. An accident. There was no blame, no guilt in it. A domestic tragedy.

Another vision has come to me recently. I call it a vision. I do not know whether it is more than that. You will know. I am falling. I am falling, my back to the water. I look up and the sun blinds me, but I can see Paul. He is above me. He is falling after me. One leg is still on the ledge but most of him is over the side. His chest scrapes against the rock on the way down and I see his skull crash into the rock and him get flipped over from the impact. A split second. And there on the ledge, through the sun, I see a head looking down at us. Yours. I saw you. The sun is behind your head, like you are an angel.

I thought I had killed him.

Perhaps I did. Perhaps I did not. If I killed him, why was I falling before him?

Your story undid me. It crept into me. I started remembering pushing him. I could picture the scene, could structure the scene. Each time I restructured the scene, more would appear. I remembered pushing him because you made me remember.

The years of silence when you said nothing to me. Was there a point at which you wanted to say something? A point at which you wanted to take it back?

Perhaps. (I give you credit.) But perhaps by then it would have been too late for us. This thing between us. It was no longer the story that was important, no longer the facts, but the telling of it, the having told it, the lingering whisper of a story that changed everything the moment it was uttered. The silence after the story that could not be broken.

There were times in my childhood I believed you

had lied, times I believed I had done nothing. Do you remember a time in the shed? I called you a liar, a murderer even. I spoke very softly, as if trying the words out. And then, later, I switched again. I might as well have done it.

I kept my distance from you. I avoided you, avoided speaking to you whenever possible. Then you left home. It was a relief. You were, I believed, keeping my secret, doing me a service. But I feared you for it. I wanted you gone. And then you left, and I thought, briefly, it might be over, but of course it was not over. You were more present in those years than ever, you might as well have been peering over my shoulder.

I do not know what really happened. I suspect the truth, but I will never know. There. It is out. You are safe. Perhaps if I lived longer, these images would form themselves into something I could identify as the truth. They have not. But I no longer believe I killed Paul. Did we slip as we jumped? Or was it you? I hope it was not. Did you run down that slope and push me and in the pushing knock Paul off balance too? Were you angry at me or did you think pushing me would be a joke? I do not know.

There is one thing I remember clearly. I will tell you. I will tell you though it will hurt. If there is anything left in you, it will hurt. Perhaps that is why I tell you. If you hurt, you are not lost.

The night Mom left, I overheard her talking to Dad.

Their door was ajar, which was why I could hear. They probably did not mean to leave it open.

Mom said – I remember each word – 'We lost all of them that day. They hate each other. They never speak.' She was crying. Dad said nothing.

There was more. She said that you knew what had happened. That you would have seen and so why would you not say anything and where did you get those cuts from anyway and what does your silence mean? I think she had tried to get you to talk to her. All those stories she read to you, putting you in situations where you could decide to tell the truth, decide to speak up. I suppose she could not just come out and ask. It would have broken her, broken her sooner.

She left that night.

That was what your story did, John. Though it was never told, other than to me, it still had that power. It changed us completely.

I wanted to go in there. Tell her not to worry. She didn't lose us, we're right here, right here in front of you. What are you talking about, we're here. We just need time. I wanted to tell her everything, tell her why we didn't speak. But then I remembered that I had murdered my brother and I did not have the courage to own up to it, and my other devoted brother was keeping a terrible secret for me, and so who was I to stand there in front of her, to be there at all. I murdered her boy. Who was I?

Do you believe me, John? Do you believe this

story? Of course you do. You were there too, you heard everything. As I walked past Paul's room, I saw you in there. You were staring out into the garden, your back to me, just staring into the black. Like some devil, John. Like some little fucking devil.

I think she knew the truth. Somehow, she knew what happened, even though she was not there. She knew what her sons were, what they were not. Dad, I am not sure about. He cast about. A good man but unable to see what was in front of him. But her – she knew.

You may ask why I have written this letter. You may ask why I did not stay to give it to you in person. It is a good question. It is a last selfish and cowardly act, you might think. Perhaps it is. Perhaps also it is one final attempt to have that story you told erased. To have it erased, I must open you up, reach inside you, wrench the heart of it out.

There is a chance it might not work. There is a chance, in ripping it out, I take you with me. The cancer, creeping around your guts, has merged with them and now you can no longer tell them apart.

I hope that is not the case. In spite of everything, you are my brother. I do not blame you for what happened. Perhaps, assuming you did push us off the ledge, your guilt was too great to allow you to face up to it. You were eight. You should not have had to bear so much at eight.

I let you down. I was, am, the older brother, I should

have done this sooner. I should have unpicked our story earlier, should have told my own story.

I do not blame you. Resent, perhaps, but not blame. I have never stopped wanting to be together again, wanting my little brother back. And perhaps this letter is the only way I can break the ice that holds us, holds you, forever in that mountain valley.

Peter.

She has read the letter so many times she has lost count. She regrets she did not open it when it was handed to her, though she does not know what she would have done had she read it while John was still in London.

When her flight is called, she gets up and goes to the gate. She is the last to board a nearly empty plane.

14

Rachel parks outside the gate of the red-brick house that belongs to her husband. To her, too, in a way, a thought she finds strange. The house is dark and she cannot see a car outside. She turns off the headlamps. As her eyes adjust, she realises it is lighter than she thought. The moon is full. She watches the shadows of leaves on the car and on the drive. She can hear crickets and the wind in the leaves. She has a sudden thought and looks to the right and left and in the rearview mirror, remembering tales of car-jackings. She looks at the trees. There could be someone there, waiting for her to get out.

The road is empty. She waits, then reaches up and switches off the interior light so that it doesn't come on when she opens the door. Eventually she gets out and presses the buzzer at the gate. There is no answer. She stands for a minute and looks out onto the road in both directions. She feels something tightening in her stomach. Not fear – something else. She can't name it. She walks up to the gates and pushes and they swing open. The noise is loud and she looks behind her, then back at the house.

She drives up to the building, keeping an eye on her rearview mirror. The gate is still open, but no one follows her.

The noise of the car door closing is loud. She is certain it will wake him if he is in the house. He was always a light sleeper. She looks at her watch. Only eight o'clock. Too early for him to be asleep.

There are no lights on and she thinks no one is home, but she rings the front-door bell anyway, hearing it echo inside the house. There is no other sound and the door does not open. She presses the bell again and steps back to look at the windows on the second storey. They are all black. No curtains.

She steps forward again and tries the handle. Locked.

She walks around the house, the grass crunching beneath her feet. At the side of the house, she goes up to a window, holds her hands around her face and peers inside. It is an empty room, small, a study perhaps. The next window she comes to is the lounge. There is nothing in there either. The moon reflects off the white walls and the concrete floors.

There is furniture in the next room, the sitting room. A chair, a table. There is something on the chair. She leans in closer to the window. It steams up with her breath which she wipes quickly away. Photographs.

There is a patio door here. She tries the handle and almost laughs when the door opens. The smell hits her: old carpet, concrete, dust. She sits on the chair, does not look around the rest of the room, and picks up the first photograph: two boys and a dog. She struggles to make it out in the light. She thinks it is a dog. It might be a mound of earth.

She does not look at the others. Instead, Rachel leans back in the chair and pulls her feet under her, rests her head against the back of the chair. She can smell him in the furniture. He has seeped into it. She closes her eyes and it is like he is there next to her, watching over her, watching her sleep.

Before she opens her eyes, she realises it is light and feels the sunlight on her face. It is warm and she feels at rest. A shadow moves across her eyes and she jumps up. There is nothing in the room or outside. She goes to the door and looks out and to the sides of the house. Nothing. She tries the handle. The door is open, but she knows she left it open. There is a key in the lock on the inside. She locks the door now, leaving the key in the lock.

She does not know why she did not explore the house last night, why she simply sat in the chair and went to sleep. He could have been upstairs. Anyone could have been upstairs. Or he could have come home. Perhaps he was out at a restaurant. It is as if she was drugged, not thinking clearly.

She listens for movement but can hear nothing.

The warmth she felt on waking has gone. As she walks through the house, she finds each room stripped bare. Unlike the first, none of the others has any furniture or carpets or curtains. The house has been swept clean, though in places there are still bits of wood, pieces of torn carpet. Somehow she knows he has done this.

Upstairs the smell is stronger. A closed-up house. Perhaps an animal, trapped inside, decomposing.

She goes into the room with the attic. She pushes the door into the attic, but it does not move. The bolt on the door is drawn but there is a keyhole too. She will look for a key later.

In the kitchen she opens the door to the garage and takes a step back when she sees the car.

Rachel feels the bonnet, though she knows the car hasn't been used for some time. It is unlocked and the keys are in the ignition. She sits in the driver's seat. On the key ring, in red letters, 'Avis'. In the cubby hole she finds documents. They have his name on them, his signature. She sits in the car with her eyes closed.

She remembers seeing the neighbouring house on the way here, though it, too, was dark. It is the only house with a view of the property. She walks round to the bungalow.

When she turns into the drive, she notices boards across the windows, the walls brown with dust. She rings the bell nonetheless and knocks too. She feels silly doing this. There is no sound and she puts her ear to the door. Nothing. She steps back. The grounds the house stands in are dry, the grass withered. She can hear crickets. There is a pot next to the front door, the plant in it long since dead. She lifts up the pot, thinking there might be a key. Nothing there, apart from a cockroach. She drops the pot and wipes her hand on her jeans. She thinks about going round to the back of the house, but something stops her, something she cannot name.

She watches the bungalow from the house next door. She

doesn't know why she does it. It is unoccupied, so there will be no one who can tell her where her husband is. But she watches in spite of this.

She stands at the window with a view of the bungalow and it is then that she sees it. The shutter swaying in the breeze. She looks at this, knowing it may be a way in, but still holds back.

She watches the house in the afternoon and into the night. She does not remain at the window. She sits on the chair downstairs, reads a book, looks at the photographs, but comes back to the window often. There is no sign of anyone.

It gets dark. She locks the doors and scans the neighbouring house for lights. There are none. The house disappears into the night and she strains to make it out.

At night, the house she is in, the one she thinks of as her husband's, grows cold. Though it is summer here, the house rattles in the wind and she feels the cold of it, the emptiness of it. She is in the corridor. Ahead of her the open doors to the bedrooms. The darkness of the corridor is broken by the light from the doors. She expects to see the shadows disturbed at any second, to see a figure emerge. A boy, she doesn't know why she expects a boy, but she can imagine him, even see him. He is shivering, most likely from the cold, though she thinks too it could be fear. The painful thing, the thing that wrenches at her, is that the boy looks like her husband. She can see him standing there in the corridor staring at her – she can see him, though she knows the corridor is empty, the rooms are empty and the house is empty too. She knows, but it makes no difference. And then she loses sight of him.

All she wants to do is find him. Find him, hold him to her. She can save him. The boy: her husband.

Rachel goes quickly through each room in the house, but he is not there. She does it again: each room. She finds herself turning around every now and then, half expecting him to be behind her. She wonders what it is in this house that makes her feel like this. She feels the weight of it, the weight of every brick pressing down on her.

Something makes her forget the room under the eaves, as if she has blocked it from her thoughts.

As she goes through the house, she opens windows and doors. She thinks about where she is, and knows she should not do this. She wouldn't do it in England, so why here? But there is something about the air in the house. If she lets the breeze blow through, perhaps she can breathe more easily.

For the first time, she notices the cameras in the corner of every room. She goes up to one, peers into it. It seems to her they are not working, though she has little experience of these things. All the same she feels watched. When she has her back to the cameras, there are prickles down her spine.

She goes downstairs and sits in the armchair. She hasn't eaten for the whole day and sleeps lightly and fitfully. Soon after dawn, she goes and stands at the fence and watches the bungalow, watches the shutter. It begins to move, shifting in slightly towards the house. She pictures a hand on the other side pulling it closed. Then it moves out again. The wind: she feels the breeze on her face. Still, though, the shutter seemed to hang longer than it should have.

She takes a couple of steps back and to the side and waits behind a tree.

Later she goes back inside, sits in the chair and reaches for the photographs. The three boys. She puts her finger on the child in the background.

There are other photographs: the back of a boy in the woods, a sleeping child, two people she thinks are her husband's parents, and a photo taken on her and John's wedding day. She looks at this for a long time.

In the early afternoon she closes her eyes and sleeps.

When she wakes, it is dark. She had not meant to sleep that long. She clutches at her face as she wakes as if it was covered in spiders' webs. The moon is bright outside the window. It lights up a patch of the floor and reaches in towards her feet. Over her shoulder, the rest of the house is dark. She listens. It creaks, settles. There is no other noise.

She walks up the stairs and goes to the room with the window overlooking the neighbour's. That house, too, is dark. She watches for a few moments, then leaves the house and begins to walk up the drive. This is probably not what a local would have done, she thinks.

She does not expect to find anyone there. In fact, she does not know what to expect and does not know why she is doing this: going to an abandoned house in a foreign country on her own. She laughs. The noise frightens her.

There is a pull that the house exerts – both houses, in fact.

She sees herself in a stream, floating on her back. Something happened here, she thinks. She drifts, hair spread out around her, down a brown river, insects buzzing in the heat.

She walks towards the window with the broken shutter. The wood is grey. The window behind it has gone. She steps closer and peers in. She can make out shapes of furniture inside, nothing else. She takes a small torch which she has found in the car and shines it into the room. The light barely reaches the door. There is a table, upturned chairs, a cabinet. On the cabinet a sole piece of china: a gravy boat. She shines the torch towards the door, but the passage beyond is dark. Nothing appears. She walks around to the back of the house.

Standing on the porch, she shines her beam towards the bungalow. There are old flowerpots, some of them overturned, and she steps around these. Then she sees the open door. She turns off the torch and listens but hears nothing. No sound at all. No insects, no night birds. Even the wind has died down. She takes a step forward and slides the door open further.

Inside, in front of the door, an old chair. To her right, a television and a laptop. There are discs on the carpet. She walks into the room, shines the torch around it. The rest of it is empty. She turns the light off and listens again.

'Hello?' Her voice sounds hollow. She stands in the doorway to the rest of the house before walking slowly down the passage. She shines the light around each room.

Back in the lounge, she flips through the discs. The ones next to the computer have dates written on them. The earliest date she finds is from soon before or after her husband must have arrived. She does not count the discs but thinks there are about forty.

She recognises the handwriting and wishes it was not his.

Rachel hesitates before tapping the keyboard. She sits on the floor, her face close to the screen. A grey light washes over her.

She jumps when she sees the face staring at her. Her husband's, but in form only. She pauses the video. She can see bones in his face she has never seen before. She tries to make out his eyes but the picture is grey and blurred. They look like pools of black. She holds her hand up to the screen and puts it on his face.

She remembers a time. Him on top of her, her hand feeling for his mouth, his breath on her palm. He kissed the hand across his mouth. She feels again the touch of his lips.

The camera points towards the door into the attic. She sees him come and go, to and from that room.

She skips over part of the disc. In the next shot, the door to the attic is open. The room inside is dark. She leans in closer to the screen. There is something there. Something hidden by the dots of the screen. Her face is against the screen. She leans back. It begins to form, forms out of the black. A man. She can see only an outline, but it is a man, of that she is sure. It is him.

He comes closer, stands in the doorframe. She watches his face disappear as he shuts the door.

The disc ends. She ejects it and examines the date. The start date is four days ago but there is no end date. She shuffles through them to find a later date. But she cannot.

Rachel backs up until she hits the chair and swivels round, still on the floor. She gets to her knees, then her feet, and runs. She stumbles as she does and trips through the open door and onto the patio and is up again and running, running away from there.

But then she stops. Where can she go? She is running from what she has seen, but running towards where it comes from. There is nowhere to go. She stops in the middle of the road.

She has to go there. He is in there. She cannot call the police, cannot wait for help. It is for her now, for her to find him, to bring him back, if that is possible.

She starts to run again, along the road and down the drive. She stumbles again and the tar cuts her. She runs through the front door and up the stairs and into the room. She runs at the door and bangs against it with the flats of her hands. It is locked and does not budge.

She scrabbles around the edges of the door, hoping it will give, as if she is the one inside wanting to get out. A coffin underground. She stops and breathes and looks around the room. She goes back downstairs and gets the axe she has seen. She comes back to the door and hesitates. Just for a second. She does not want to see what she knows is in there.

The smell of the house, the stink of it. The feeling of not being alone.

She raises the axe over her shoulder. It takes several blows before she makes a hole in the door. She looks through it but can see nothing. She puts her hand through the hole and feels for the key, half expecting another hand to reach out for hers.

She can see it clearly, feel it even – a child's hand. Again, she does not know why she expects a child.

She finds a bolt. There is no lock on it. She pulls it back and the door opens inwards. The smell hits her. The smell of the house comes from this room.

It is black inside. She notices pinpricks of light. Gaps in the roof tiles. She notices these first and they are like stars and then the room grows lighter. But one area does not grow lighter. A shape begins to form. The room lightens around it.

She does not step into the room. She cannot do that. She thinks she sees it move. It is moving, crawling slowly towards her.

'John.'

15

Rachel Hyde watches as they load her husband into the back of an ambulance. He seems smaller – like a child. The police cars have their lights on still. They flash blue against the house. She wonders why they do this, what the point is.

The ambulance driver told her where they would take John. She did not ask to go with him. She is not sure she wants that and is ashamed to feel that way.

She thinks of him, huddled in the corner of the room, and remembers the fear on seeing him, fear of this man and everything he might have done, everything he might be. But what exactly has he done? Can she be sure he has done something? Did he lie? He was eight. Everyone lies. Did he push his brothers off a cliff, sending one to his death? If he did that, then did he mean to? There is no way for her to know.

She came here to find her husband. She has found him. But he is not who she set out to find. He is a mass of bones and flesh and hidden somewhere inside, something she has never known, never been allowed to see.

The letter opened the wound and here – there – when she opened the door, she saw the insides of it, the rotting, stinking flesh of it.

When the ambulance drives off, she walks upstairs to the room where she found him. Already the smell has started to go. Now there is a smell of something else instead: the bodies of the police and forensics team. The room seems smaller as well, much smaller with all these people inside, and with the lights they have set up.

A mirror is propped against the wall. He was slouched opposite it when she found him. She can imagine him watching himself in it. If you examine a mystery closely enough, for long enough, certainty will follow. Certainty, but not necessarily truth. This is what she finds herself thinking.

Later, a man comes to talk to her.

'I am Major Mbuli.'

She says nothing.

'The man, John Hyde, is your husband?'

'Yes.'

'He has been here for all this time?'

She shakes her head, confused.

'In Port Elizabeth, I mean.'

'We are, were, separated.'

The man nods. 'Have you spoken to him in the last few months?'

She shakes her head.

'I have met him before.'

She looks up at this.

'He found the body. Of his brother, I mean.'

'I did not know that.' She pauses. 'How did he die?'

'He hanged himself. In the same room where you found your husband.'

She holds her voice steady. 'There was a letter. He would have known, would have guessed what his brother was going to do.'

'Yes.' The policeman's tone changes. 'He phoned. I am afraid to say the message did not get through.'

'Did not get through?'

'The message was not relayed. Later we sent a car, but it was too late. Mr Hyde had beaten us to it.'

Rachel wonders which Hyde he means.

'I am sorry. There have been cuts.' He goes on. 'You have the letter? Mr Hyde was not able to produce it.'

'Do you suspect him of something?'

'We did at first, but he was on a plane, somewhere over Africa at the time it happened. Nothing to answer for.'

'Nothing to answer for? Are you sure?'

'What do you mean?'

She shakes her head. 'Nothing. I do not have it. The letter, I mean.'

Mbuli nods. He does not press it. 'Your husband will live. That's what they tell me. He is severely dehydrated, but you found him in time. Another day, and ...' He pauses. 'We will need you to come and give a statement. But there is no rush.'

He turns to go, but then stops. 'You did not know Mr Hyde? Peter Hyde, I mean.'

She shakes her head. 'I only met him once.'

He nods. 'I am sorry.'

He leaves. She does not know what he is sorry for.

She does not go to the hospital the next day and does not call. Instead, she goes to the house next door. She watches the DVDs almost without stopping. She does not watch everything on them – that is impossible. Instead, she watches most of them using fast-forward.

She watches him paint the house, and then, later, much later, remove the furniture and carpets. She watches a speck disappear in the garden and the smoke that follows.

She sees him leave the larger house and walk in the direction of the fence. The camera loses sight of him, but she knows he was coming here to the bungalow. He does this many times.

She sees him sitting in the chair in the larger house, hand resting over the side. He jerks. She thinks at first he has fallen asleep and the movement was him waking. But she can see his eyes and they remain open. She watches his hand, held rigid over the arm of the chair.

She sees John sleeping, moonlight washing over him. He gets out of bed while it is still dark and leaves the room. She can see only shadows. He does this several times. It may be sleepwalking. She is not sure.

He is in the corridor, sitting with his back to the wall. She can see his head move, back and forth. He seems to be hitting it against the wall. She turns up the volume, but the only sound is the buzzing from the television itself. She looks closer. His face, from what she can see, is in a grimace. She thinks he is crying.

He stands at a window looking out at the garden and does not move. She checks the player to be sure, but there is nothing wrong with it. She checks the time. He stands in the same position for eight hours, the only movement the tapping of his fingers on his leg. The window faces the front garden and the road. She wonders what was out there, though she suspects she knows the answer.

He runs through the house, from room to room. There is no reason to it.

She watches the last disc again. Watches the black space where she knows her husband chose to die.

Then she stops. She begins arranging the discs in date order. As she does this, she notices another disc under the chair. This has different handwriting on it and is dated earlier than any of the others. On this one she sees Peter. The face from the park. She sees him in the room under the eaves and she sees him place a rope over the beam and she watches him hanging from the beam until he stops swinging and the camera stops. The next image is of her husband bursting into the room. On the disc this happens a second after Peter hangs himself, but she knows it could have been days. She sees him launch himself at the body, sees him hold it up and try to grab the rope. He has to let go and he runs down the stairs and gets a knife and comes back and cuts the rope and she sees his brother fall at his feet. John loosens the rope and he takes his brother's face in his hands and he kneels there with him, rocking back and forth, and she can see that he is shouting at the body, shouting so much his neck muscles strain, she can see them even in the grainy picture. She watches him do this until there is no more space on the DVD and it goes back to the beginning and she sees Peter's face fill the screen as if nothing had happened.

She drives to the library and looks at newspapers from 1983. She starts with the twelfth of December, but there is nothing. In a copy dated the thirteenth, though, she finds a short article, a matter of a few lines: 'Paul Hyde, aged ten, a resident of Kragga Kamma, died in an accident in the mountains near Barrydale. He leaves his father, mother and two brothers, aged eight and twelve.' That is all.

She also goes to the police station. She finds Mbuli there and she leaves the discs. She explains where she found them. The policeman does not look surprised. Perhaps it is his training.

'Will there be charges?'

'He has done nothing wrong.'

She nods.

When she returns to Peter's house – she finds it hard now to think of it as John's house – she looks again at the photograph of his parents. She is struck by how alike they look. John and his father. His father wears a broad grin. She finds herself smiling, but stops when she realises what she is doing.

She finds the letter from his father. It is back in the envelope in the drawer. Now she knows more. She would not say she understands it. It is not for her to understand.

Also in the drawer is a man's watch. She turns it over and reads the date inscribed there. She holds it for a long time. Night has fallen before she can bear to put it down. It is something to hold on to.

16

He does not belong in this country. He is free to leave and he will. The past that belongs to him, that he has made his own, has seen to that. The stories told have seeped into the country around him. They clutch at his feet and drag him down, pin him here. He wants to leave. But he cannot. Not yet.

If he could somehow take the story he told, or the story he did not tell, and bury it under a rock in the middle of the Karoo, walk away and forget where it was hidden, then maybe, just maybe, he could stay. He could stay here, unfettered, in a virgin country, a new life, Rachel at his side.

He has put the house up for sale for almost nothing. The bungalow next door too. He cannot go back to the house. He knows that. And perhaps someone else can make something of it. Someone, wanting to live out there, will choose it out of the six or seven nearby also for sale. It won't be the same for them. It is just a house after all: brick, cement.

It is his final betrayal: selling the house his father would not sell. But he knows, too, this is what his father would have wanted. For his son to be free of it all. It is why he did not call him back until the end.

He still sees them. He has not told anyone this. He still sees them, but not like before – his father, his mother, Paul and Peter. The shape of a head in a crowd, a glimpse out of the corner of his eye of one of them looking at him. He went for a walk in the park a few days ago with Rachel and, in the distance, walking hand in hand with an adult, he recognised Paul, the child's head half-turned. It was far away but he knew it was him.

He kept it to himself. His hold on Rachel's hand did not tighten. He is certain of that. He is certain, though he also knows he blacked out for a second, was somewhere else entirely. These periods have been getting shorter. They are almost gone. It is only a matter of time.

He looked at Rachel then, walking alongside him. He noticed the lines on her face. He pulled her towards him and she gave him half a smile. It is important she does not notice. It is important, for a reason beyond himself, a reason he is beginning to understand, that he does not let go of her again, that his past does not weigh on her.

That she knows is a comfort to him, one he did not expect. He knows she wants children. He thinks he may be ready, and ready to offer more too. Peter. Or Neil. Or Paul. Sarah if it is a girl. If indeed she will want those names now that she knows. In some ways he thinks it may be better not to have those names – but only in some ways.

She has agreed to a trip before they fly home, before they restart their lives in England. She wondered if it was a good idea. He knows it may be the worst idea he could have had, but at the same time he knows that his story is not complete. He needs to go to where it started, stand there, and let it seep through him, to see what remains behind. That is his hope. It is the only way he knows how to bury those words, 'I saw'. It is the only way he knows to get back to the moment, the moment they went off the edge.

That moment is still lost. Though John knows he was responsible, he does not know why and cannot remember the seconds before. The doctors told Peter he might never remember, but they did not say the same to him. The doctors did not tell him, did not warn him, that in changing the story for someone else he would change it for himself too, and the true story would be replaced by this other, this doppelgänger.

He has not seen the other boy. This gives him little comfort.

At George, it begins to rain. He slows down. The rain stops three hours later as they turn off the N2 towards Barrydale. There is still mist in the air.

The first stretch of this road is flat, but then they begin to climb and the mist grows thicker. He struggles to see more than a few metres ahead and is driving at the speed he would drive in a city. The mist collects in drops on the windscreen. He looks out of the window on his left, looking for the place. He remembers it clearly. Or he thinks he does. It was almost twenty-nine years ago now. He remembers they parked alongside the road at a viewpoint. Opposite, the mountain was covered in yellow flowers. The flowers are out again, though the weather is different. They climbed over the wall and there was a path leading down to the pools. He remembers that it could not be seen from the road. Not a path as such. He remembers branches scratching his skin.

He passes one stop. It does not look familiar. Then another. He drives another two kilometres further into the mountains. Each stopping place is no more familiar than the last. He tries to remember which side of the pass it was, but nothing. He stops, not because he thinks it is the place but because he has to choose one.

He looks across at the mountains. They are swathed in mist so thick it is like rain. It billows across the valley. The flowers he remembers, the smell too. There is one smell: rain, tar, gravel. There is another as well: the mountain itself, the mineral, metallic taste of it. He remembers the dirt in his mouth when he fell as a boy.

'Is it here?'

He shrugs. 'I'll take a look.' She makes no movement to get out of the car and instead just nods. He is grateful for that.

He walks along the wall, looking for the path he remembers. He sees tins, a crisp packet, cigarette ends. There is no obvious path. He looks back at the car and at her in it. It is covered in drops of water. Dust too. The raindrops make paths through the dust. He can barely see her, though he knows she is looking at him. The rain and mud run through her face.

He turns away and looks back down the valley slope. He

knows he would not be able to see the pools from here. He pauses. He knows what he should do: climb over, find the path and if it is not there, then drive on.

He sits on the wall. The mist collects on his arms and he watches the drops cling to his hairs. He wipes one finger across his forearm and the water runs off. He can feel it seeping into his clothes now. He looks down the side of the valley again, gets up and steps over the wall.

He walks along the edge of the fynbos on the other side of the wall. There is no gap, no obvious way down. He retraces his steps and goes in the opposite direction. At one point there is a space between two branches. He can see the space continue a little way down the mountainside before it disappears behind a boulder. Not a path as such, but perhaps it once was. Used just enough now to keep the route visible. He wonders if there was ever a proper path. To the boys it might have seemed so as they were small, but not to the parents. They just pushed a way through.

The bush scratches his hands and tears at his trousers. A thorn leaves a line of blood. It mingles with the water. He likes this. Something about being this close to the bush, feeling it inside him, feeling the water trickle into his shoes. He is soaked through by now with the mist and the water on the bush, but he makes no move to lift his arms free.

He feels nothing familiar, as if moving further into the mountains has drowned the memories, drowned the smell.

From behind the rock, he can see the way downhill. He looks back and to the right. The road, the car, the wall have all disappeared already. He hears a car, but it does not stop and the noise seems far away. At that moment, standing behind the rock, hearing the car go by, something hits him. He wants to call it a memory. It is more a vision than a memory. He sees it, but as if it happens to someone else, happened to someone else.

He sees them, more clearly now than at any time since he left the house. It frightens him. He thinks of turning back, but he cannot lie to Rachel. Not again. He should not have brought her.

His father is in the lead, striding ahead through the bush, carrying a basket. He pushes his way through the bush, not caring about the scratches, breaking branches, clearing a way for the others to follow. After him, the two older boys: Peter in front, then Paul. There are towels over their shoulders.

He, the boy he knows is himself, carries a camera. Hyde watches him. His heart is beating a little faster at the sight of him but he breathes in deeply. He picks his way more carefully through the bushes and is a little way behind his brothers and behind his mother too. He watches as his mother holds a branch to one side for him. 'Come on.' He hears the words now, as clearly as twenty-nine years ago. The gesture is gentle, the words are not. He can see the sweat on her face. They push their way through the bush, now as tall as them, and they are gone. The noise of their feet, their voices, vanish. He hears the call of a bird.

He starts after them, parting the bushes with his arms. After a few minutes he emerges into a clearing. There are rocks and through them runs the river. His parents are there too. They are setting up the picnic, putting out blankets on rocks. Now they stand, looking downstream to the pools. They stand with their backs to him, unmoving. He cannot see the children.

He moves out of the last of the bushes and approaches them. He realises there is no sound. The water flows by, but he can hear nothing. He looks up. The mist is even lower. There is a grey cloth further up the mountainside that will be covering the road. He has descended through it. He thinks of Rachel and he calls out, but nothing comes from his chest and he knows anyway she wouldn't be able to hear him. Not here. Not now.

It is as if he is under water. The air is thick around him, thick and wet. He heads towards his mother and father. Still they don't move. He sees their faces in profile. His father, the same age he is now, looks down the river. There is a breeze, just one breath. It picks up his hair. His mother's too. She stands on his father's right, slightly behind him. He sees the wrinkles in the corner of her eye. She squints. There is no sun today. Neither of them are smiling. His father's mouth is half open. Is he calling out? Is he talking to his wife? Perhaps he has just sworn, just realised, half-realised, what is happening further downstream.

His mother's hands are halfway up to her face. Cupping her hands around her mouth to call out. Or just finished. The skin of her neck stretched out by the grimace of her lips.

He walks between them now, inches away. He stands in front of them, his back to the waterfall. He wants to reach out to them, wants to hold their hands, to be held by them. Most of all he wants to push them back, back away from here, back up the slope and back into the Chevrolet baking in the sun.

He reaches out to them.

They move.

Their heads swivel. Their gaze shifts from the middle distance to his face. Their lips close, their faces blank. He sees something in their gazes, though. He sees that they know, that they are filled with the knowledge of what he has done, of what he will do.

They stare at him and he turns and begins to run. He crashes into the bush, not following a path, and runs through it. Lines of blood appear on his skin.

After some time he stops and tries to gather his breath. There are steep drops around here. The parents told the children that. They told them. He needs to be careful where he puts his feet.

He looks out over the bush. The flowers on the bush are at neck height – a carpet of yellow. The bush. The mountain. It is raining now and it falls in swathes but he cannot feel the breeze. He crouches. Down here there are no leaves. He can see through the branches, across the ground. He looks to his left, off the path, up the mountain, and to his right. He sees something that makes him stand upright again. Just two metres away, he sees legs from the knee down. The branches and leaves cut off the rest of them. The legs of a child. He stands up and calls out 'Hello?' He does not expect an answer. He crouches again, but they are gone. He scans the bush to the left and right, looks ahead and behind. Nothing. He gets up. Off the path, a few metres away, further down the hill, the bushes sway. First one bush moves, then another, as if something slithers between them. He plunges into the bush again, following the child he can see, the child he thinks he sees, running through the bush, flitting between leaves and branches.

His feet slip. Once he finds himself falling and stays upright by grabbing the branches. He stops then and scans the bush. It is still again. A drop of rain gathers on his eyelash. He blinks to get rid of it, feels the salt from his skin in his eye. It makes his eye water and a tear rolls down his cheek.

There, to his right, another movement. He bends down below the leaf cover, but can see nothing. He runs again, following the swaying branches.

He stops, focuses on his breathing. Tells himself what he is seeing is not real. He trusts in the logic of it. He tells himself to hold back from this, not to fall again.

When he stops, the swaying stops. He waits, crouched in silence. The only noise now the river. It is closer, but still some distance off. He grabs a branch and shakes it. It soaks him. There is a ripple further off as he shakes the branch. He takes a step closer, stops. The swaying stops too. He shakes a branch, it starts again. He waits for it to die down. He feels his heart in his chest. There, ahead and to the right, a ripple, this time not of his making. It seems to be coming towards him. He stands rooted. The branches press against his chest, his arms hang by his side. He watches the movement. It comes right up to him, right up to the leaves in front of him. He waits and he can sense hands reaching out to him, reaching out to grab his own hands, his legs. His flesh tingles. He wants to duck down into the branches and put his face right up against the face of the child beneath, and cry out to him, shout as loud as he can in the face of one so close, yet who is too far away to hear, scream at him to stop, to stop what he is about to do. He stands. His head goes back, his face tilts to the rain, his eyes close. He waits for the child to take him.

Then he senses the child turn around and move off. He feels the absence, the withdrawing. He opens his eyes and sees movement straight ahead and Hyde is running again, running, though the branches stick in his flesh and hold him back. They stick and tear, and as he moves he feels as if he leaves bits of him behind. Stripped to the bone, his flesh hung out on branches to dry. Votives to the gods.

And now he is a boy again. As he runs, leaving his flesh behind, he grows smaller and the bush swallows him. He bursts onto a path, a narrow line of stones running through the bush and he is running, running and slipping and falling, and the only way he knows how to stop falling again is to run faster and faster, but he cannot stop himself falling and his legs are moving but not touching the ground and then the stones disappear and the bush on either side falls away and he is out, free of the bush, the ledge a little way down the path, free, light as air.

He sees them in front of him. For a second he is stopped. Mid-air. Floating in the sky. Things come to him then, memories of times before this moment: the slights, the pushes, the dead dog in the road, the scorecard fluttering out of the window. Moments of nothing. He feels a hardening in his chest when he sees them, when these things come back, and he goes inside and he wants to know what it is, wants to know what he was thinking then as he hurtles towards his brothers, whether he can remember what he was thinking, remember what it is he wanted to do, what he thought he wanted to do. Was he trying to stop? Did he think it would be funny, would get him back in their good books if he pushed one of them off, did he want both of them gone because that would teach them, was he thinking only of trying to stop, trying to stop his own flight over the edge of a cliff? Was it one of these or all of them? He tries to feel in the remembering of this moment whether he could stop, could have stopped.

He is running again, flying again, his feet have still not touched the ground, and he is so close to them, so close he can feel the warmth from their skin.

At the moment they touch, time stops again, or slows. He feels his hand placed on Peter's back, his other on Paul's shoulder, his head somewhere between them. He feels a brush on his cheek, the skin of one of them. He tries to remember the next moment, what happened in his own arms, hands, torso. He wills his body to repeat the moment, wills his muscles to remember what it is they were trying to do – stop one fall or start another – in that very second that Peter and Paul went over.

But it is gone.

Peter and Paul are flying. Children launched into the blue.

John, the boy, his hands and knees cut, is sprawled on the ledge, legs sticking out into space, clinging to the rock by his fingernails. For a second he thought he too was going over.

He is alone, on his back. He looks up into the sky. Bright sunshine. He looks up and he stares at the sun. He opens his eyes and he stares at the sun and does not close his eyes, does not close them until he can bear it no longer. When he does close them, there, burnt on the inside of him, burnt there forever, the flight of his brothers, whom he loves more than anything, though he has not known it until then, and never allowed himself to remember it until then.

He is singing. Not out loud – under his breath. Breathless. It is a nursery rhyme. He is singing to himself as if it could make everything go away, as if concentrating on the words, bringing them to life could make everything else go away. Come back, Peter. Come back, Paul.

The man is flying too. He has left his child self behind on the ledge.

As he falls, he jumps out at the same time. He knows what will happen if he does not; if, instead, he falls straight down.

He hangs, suspended in the thick air. It is silent.

And then – it feels like a lifetime – the cold, the shock of the cold, as he plunges into the river. He drinks it in. He kicks, not sure which way is up. He opens his eyes and he can see nothing except brown water and the white flecks created by his fall.

He breathes in water.

He feels himself sinking. Though his lungs are full of air, he feels heavy. It is a slow process. He sinks like a dead fish. He feels the weight of the water on him, pressing against his ears. He floats, face pointing at the surface, arms to the side.

He opens his eyes slowly as if waking from a deep sleep. The boy in front of him floats into vision. His hair floats around his face. The boy's eyes, like his own a moment ago, are closed. Light dances on his cheeks. An air bubble escapes from his nose. The man follows it until it disappears against the surface of the water.

He looks back at the boy and he does not shy away from what he sees. He looks at it, looks it in the face. The water is darker around his face, like a cloth, a blanket holding him. The darkness spreads from the side of his head. A flap of skin moves in the current. The head itself at an angle it never took in life.

He comes to him. Paul comes towards him, walking through the water. John stares at him. It is as if he has seen him just yesterday – the face, the eyes. They stare back and almost three decades vanish. They are boys once again, running across a sun-bleached garden, their laughter whipped away by the wind.

Hyde is struck by the beauty of him. Though the lips and skin are blue, he is struck by the beauty of the vanished boy.

The boy takes another step forward. Hyde can smell him. A dead boy carries a particular smell, is the thought that comes to him. One thought in a darkened space. Spring water, rotting leaves, young blue skin.

Hyde waits, closes his eyes, waits to be taken. Instead, a hand reaches out to him. It reaches out and touches the top of his head. He can feel the coldness, the dampness of it, even through the water. The hand reaches out to him and is laid on top of his head and as it lies there, Hyde feels a warmth begin and feels it spread in that touch, a warmth he could never have imagined.

John Hyde pulls himself out of the pool. His foot slips on a weed-covered rock and he gulps more water, but manages on the second attempt. He lies on his back on the rock, his head turned towards the pool. He watches as the surface calms.

He stares into the grey above him, the mist thicker now. There, on the ledge, barely visible in the mist, he sees himself as a boy again. It is just an outline, the figure disappearing. But even as it disappears into the mist, John remembers standing there, getting up after the fall. He remembers standing there, looking down at what he had done, knowing, somehow, what he had done already, not needing to see the evidence. He remembers the warmth of the urine running down his legs and how, when he moved his foot, there was a wet footprint, and how he focused on this until it dried in the sun, and he remembers the feeling in his chest, what he can now describe only as fear, though it is something more than that, the fear that no eight-year-old should have, that comes with knowing that what he has done, whatever the reason, has broken the world and can never be spoken of.

He is alone again. The boy has gone into the mist. A single bird calls.

He will go back up there, back to the woman in the car waiting for him. He will go back because it is what he must do now, what is given to him to do. It is all he can ever do.

He hears the rushing of the river. He can almost hear it cleansing the mountainside. The rocks, silt, plants, bodies of animals, the memory of what these things used to be, hurtling down the mountain. They slow down, the river widens, until, after some distance, it empties into the sea and the water there is turned brown near the shoreline before the river and everything in it is lost, swallowed by an immensity that pays it no heed.

Acknowledgements

Thank you to Geoff Mulligan for his insightful and sensitive editing and to all at Clerkenwell Press. Thanks also to Fourie Botha and Random House Struik. Dr Natalie Clarke and David and Melanie Bruce helped with aspects of the research. Any mistakes are, of course, mine. Throughout the writing of the novel I benefitted from the close reading, critique and suggestions of Andrew McIntosh. Finally, thank you, as ever, to Tabatha, Sophia and Elliot.